Pups that Make Miracles

Therapy dogs work their magic this Christmas!

Welcome to Christmas at Heatherglen Clinic!

Set in a beautiful castle, nestled in the Highlands of Scotland, it's the perfect place for patients to recover and rehabilitate from their injuries.

The medical professionals working at this exclusive estate are dedicated to mending their patients, but the magic of this special place and the clinic's adorable four-legged therapy partners help heal even the most broken of hearts and bring happily-ever-afters to both staff and patients alike!

Discover how healing pups help make Christmas miracles happen in this brand-new miniseries guaranteed to leave paw prints on your heart!

Highland Doc's Christmas Rescue
by Susan Carlisle

Festive Fling with the Single Dad
by Annie Claydon

Available now!

Making Christmas Special Again
by Annie O'Neil

Their One-Night Christmas Gift
by Karin Baine

Coming next month!

Dear Reader,

I love to travel and this book gave me a chance to go to Scotland. To write a Scotsman's story was even better. Who doesn't like a handsome man with a great accent? Lyle, the hero in this book, has all of that in spades. Cass, the woman he falls in love with, isn't immune to his charm either. I hope you enjoy Lyle and Cass's story and the holiday season in Scotland.

I also want to say how much I have enjoyed working with Annie O'Neil, Annie Claydon and Karin Baine on this continuity. These women are great and they only make me look better. You don't want to miss a single book in this continuity. A Scottish Christmas is like no other.

Please join my newsletter list at susancarlisle.com and get all the latest news on my books. I'd love to hear from you.

Susan

HIGHLAND DOC'S CHRISTMAS RESCUE

SUSAN CARLISLE

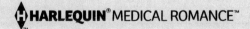

ISBN-13: 978-1-335-64189-2

Highland Doc's Christmas Rescue

First North American Publication 2019

Copyright © 2019 by Susan Carlisle

To Dallas

I'm proud of the man you are, and your father would be also.

CHAPTER ONE

As THE TAXI rolled up the rise Cass Bellow looked out the window at the snow-blanketed Heatherglen Castle Clinic in northern Scotland. Why had she been sent here?

More than once she'd questioned her doctor's wisdom in transferring her to this private clinic for physical therapy. Weren't there plenty of other places in warmer climates? Particularly in her native US. Or, better yet, couldn't she have just gone home and handled what needed doing on her own? But, no, her doctor insisted she should be at Heatherglen. Had stated that he sent all his patients with extensive orthopedic injuries there. He declared the place was her best hope for a full recovery. Finally, at her argument, he'd bluntly told her that if she wanted him to sign off on her release she must complete her physical therapy at Heatherglen.

As the car came to a stop at the front door

she studied the Norman architecture of the building with its smooth stone walls and slate roof. The place was huge, and breathtaking. There were more chimneys than Cass had a chance to count. This place was nothing like what she'd expected. Though it was early November, festive Christmas wreaths made of greenery and red bows already hung on the outside of the lower floor windows. They further darkened her mood.

When she had been given the search and rescue assignment assisting the military after an explosion in Eastern Europe, she had never dreamed she'd end up in traction in an army hospital on a base in Germany. Her shattered arm and leg had finally mended, but she needed physical therapy to regain complete use of them. Now she'd been sent to this far-flung, snowy place to do just that. All she really wanted was to be left alone.

She opened the cab door and wind blasted her. Despite the heat coming from the still running car, she shuddered. As Cass stepped out, one of the large wooden castle doors, decked with a huge Christmas wreath full of red berries, opened. A tall man, perhaps in his mid-thirties, with the wide shoulders of an athlete stepped out. With rust-colored hair and wearing a heavy tan cable sweater and dark brown pants, he looked like the epitome of what she thought a Scottish man should be. As he came down the few steps toward her, he smiled.

"Hello, you must be Ms. Cassandra Bellow. I'm Dr. Lyle Sinclair, the medical director here at Heatherglen. You may call me Lyle."

His thick Scottish brogue confirmed her earlier thoughts. Yet she was surprised by the way the sunny cheerfulness of his voice curled around her name, nudging at her icy emotions. Irritated, she pushed that odd notion away. This doctor was far too happy and personable for her taste. Her goal was to do what must be done with as little interaction with others as possible. She planned on nursing her wounds in private.

"Yes, that's me." To her satisfaction her flat, dry tone dropped the brightness of his smile a notch. If she could just get to her room and collapse she'd be happy. Her right side was burning from the ache in her arm and the agony of putting her full weight on her right leg.

"Flora McNeith, the physiotherapist whose care you'll be under, couldn't be here to greet you and asked that I get you settled in." Concern filled his face. "Do you need a wheelchair? Crutches?"

"No, I can walk on my own. Run, that's another thing." She pulled at her jacket to stop the biting flow of air down her neck.

A light chuckle rolled out of his throat and over her nerve endings. "I understand. Then let's get inside out of this weather." He looked up at the sky. A snowflake landed on the dark red five o'clock shadow covering his cheek.

Cass averted her eyes and gave the cobblestone drive, cleared of snow, a searching look. It was farther than she wanted to walk, yet she wouldn't let on. The three steps up to the door looked even more daunting.

All she needed was fortitude to make the walk and climb those steps. She had plenty of that. Soft snowflakes continued to drift down as she took a deep breath and steeled herself to put one foot in front of the other. With another silent inhalation, she started toward the entrance. Dr. Sinclair walked beside her.

She managed the first two steps with no mishap but the toe of her short boot caught the edge of the last one. Grabbing at air, Cass finally found the fabric covering Dr. Sinclair's arm. She yelped with the effort to hold on. Being right-handed, she'd instinctively flailed out that arm and immediately regretted it. Pain shot through it, but not as sharp as it had been weeks earlier. She gritted her teeth, thrusting out her other arm to ease the fall.

Instead of tumbling onto the steps, her body was brought against a hard wall of human torso. The doctor's arm circled her waist and held her steady. Her face smashed into thick yarn. A hint of pine and smoke filled her nose. For some reason it was reassuring.

"Steady on, I've got you." His deep burr was near her ear.

Cass quickly straightened, getting her feet under her even though pain rocked her. She refused to show it, having already embarrassed herself enough. Her lips tightened. "I'm fine. Thank you."

Glancing at him, she got the weirdest impression that the concern in his eyes had nothing to do with her physical injuries, as if he was able to see her true pain. That was a crazy idea. She shook that odd thought off and focused on where she was.

Taking a third fortifying breath, Cass stepped into the massive foyer.

No way was she going to let him see the effort it took to keep walking. She'd lived through much worse. She'd always been self-sufficient. Weakness wasn't in her vocabulary. As a young girl she had learned the power of being emotionally strong.

Still, that brief human contact had been nice. There were two enormous cement urns

filled with pine and berries on either side of
the doors. Cass looked further to see the stone
arched beams of the ceiling then on to a grand
staircase. On the floor beside it lay a pile of
pine wood. Here she was in this strange place
for the holidays when all she wished for was
home. She would get her arm and leg strong
again as fast as she could, then return to America to grieve her loss in private.

"Are you sure you're okay?" The doctor
stood too close as if he was afraid she might
stumble again.

"I'm fine." The words sounded sharp and
overly loud in the cavernous entrance hall. If
she could just get to her room, she could nurse
the excruciating throbbing in her arm and leg.
She would be limping by then as well.

"On our way to your room, let me tell you
where a few things are. This is Admissions."
He waved a hand to indicate a room off the
hall. "Louise, my administrative assistant, and
I have our offices there. She's out this afternoon as well. You two can sort out the paperwork in the morning. I'm sure you're tired."

Cass was beyond tired. The effort it had
taken her to travel from Germany to Fort William then the drive north had worn her out.
She hadn't recovered anywhere near as much
as she wanted to believe.

"Over here is the dining room." He walked across the hall and stood in a wide doorway.

Cass joined him. Despite her physical distress, she loved his accent. It was soothing, for some reason.

The room he wanted her to see was long and wide with a dark barrel ceiling sculpted out of wood from which hung large, black iron chandeliers. A fireplace Cass could stand up in filled the wall on the far end with flags arranged overhead. The walls were partially covered in wainscoting. Above that were a few male portraits in impressive frames. A huge table, surrounded by imposing matching chairs, capable of seating at least twenty people, stood in the center of the room. An oriental rug in blue and red lay beneath it. The only thing out of place was a pile of greenery on the floor in one corner and a few boxes stacked beside it.

He must have noticed the direction of her gaze. "Pardon the mess. We're in the process of decorating for Christmas."

Cass pretended he hadn't spoken. Not even the holidays could heal her broken heart.

Dr. Sinclair was saying, "All meals are served here, unless there's a reason the resident is incapable of joining us. We dress for the evening meal. It's at seven."

"Dress? As in diamonds and tux?"

Chuckling, he shook his head. "No. More like no workout clothes allowed. The idea is for the residents to use their skills and have something positive to look forward to. We work on the principle that if you don't use it, you lose it."

She glanced at him. He really was quite handsome in a rugged way. "Like?"

"Fastening a button, passing a bowl or even manipulating a fork." He turned toward the central hall.

"I have no trouble with any of those so why must I attend?" She joined him.

"Because we want our residents to feel like they're part of our family, which they are," he said over his shoulder as he started down the hall.

She had zero interest in being sociable. All she wanted was time to herself to think about what she would do next, where she wanted her life to go. How she could get past the mass of emotions churning inside her. Could she continue working in search and rescue? Work with a new dog? Learn to trust another man?

Maybe she could just make sure she wasn't around when it was dinnertime. This place sounded more like a prison than a clinic. "Hey, do you mind telling me why I was sent here?"

That got his attention. "So you can regain your mobility."

"I know that. I mean why here in particular? Couldn't I have gone to a clinic in America? What makes this place so special?"

He shoved his hands into his pockets. "As I understand it, your orthopedic doctor believes this is the right clinic for you."

She stepped toward him, pinning him with a direct look. "What led him to believe this specific clinic was the right place for me to complete my physical therapy?"

Dr. Sinclair shifted his weight and raised his chin. "I'm not sure what you're looking for but our residents have an uncommonly high success rate of making as complete a recovery as possible, and by recovery I mean holistic recovery. Our state-of-the-art clinic features a peaceful atmosphere conducive to healing…" he waved a hand around, indicating the castle "…and our canine therapy has proved to be fundamental in facilitating that recovery as well. Does that reassure you?"

Canine therapy. Cass took a step back, her chest constricting. She couldn't deal with this right now. It was too soon after the loss of her dog and partner, Rufus. "I'm not interested in canine therapy."

Her German shepherd-wolfhound mix partner had been with her for four years. She'd had him since he was a puppy. She'd even gone to Germany to pick him up from the breeders. They had trained together at a search and rescue school in California. They'd understood each other, trusted one another.

Now he was gone. Despite him being an animal, the hurt of his loss was more acute than the pain of broken bones or her ex-boyfriend's assessment of her ability to maintain a relationship. She and Rufus had been all over the world together, crawling in and over disaster sites that others only saw on TV while drinking their morning coffee. As a team, they had been a part of tragedies that no one should ever see or experience. Gratitude and guilt filled her in equal measure.

She felt the doctor's keen observation and focused on his mild expression. He turned and started down an adjacent hall to the left, saying, "This way to the lift."

Cass glanced at the staircase in relief then followed, taking careful steps to ensure there wasn't a repeat performance of what had almost happened outside.

He looked over his shoulder. "As our residents improve, they use the stairs whenever possible."

Cass once more eyed the daunting set of

wide steps made of gray marble. "And that's mandatory?"

Dr. Sinclair gave her a grin. "'Mandatory' is such an unfriendly word. Why don't we go with 'greatly encouraged'? It's part of the graduation program to be able to walk up and down the stairs, but we don't require that until you're ready."

Did her relief show on her face? "What makes you think I'm not ready?"

"Maybe the tight line of your lips that indicates that little stumble outside hurt more than you wish to admit."

Cass grimaced inwardly. The man had an acute sense of awareness. Could he see that more than her body pained her? That her heart hurt? Cass hoped not. She was nowhere near ready to share her feelings. "I don't hurt."

"Liar." He gave her a flash of a smile. One she was sure made people want to confide in him, which she wasn't going to do. As if he knew what she was thinking, he said in a gentle manner, "You do know it isn't weakness to admit you're in pain or that you need help. That's what we're here for."

She'd had enough of this. All she wanted was to get to her room. "Who're you, the resident shrink?"

They walked out of the elevator and started

down a wide hallway lined with portraits. A few decorations were already in place here and there. A red carpet runner muffled their steps.

"No, but as clinic administrator and emergency medical doctor I help develop the patients' therapy. All the doctors here work together to form patient plans. Recovery is as much mental as it is physical."

"So you think I have emotional issues?" Cass certainly did have them. She couldn't keep her job without a dog, and she wasn't sure she could handle having another one. To possibly lose another best friend would be too much, too painful. To get close enough that someone or something mattered was more than she wanted at this point.

Lyle's…wasn't that his name?…mouth quirked as he stopped to face her.

"Why, Ms. Bellow, in some ways I think everyone has issues. So don't go thinking you're special. Here we are." He pushed open a thick wooden door. "Your room belonged to the lady of the castle."

Cass couldn't deny it was a grand room. Its large canopy bed was hung with seafoam green curtains and covered with a matching spread. Beneath a bank of windows was a seating arrangement of a loveseat and two cushioned chairs. A chest, which she guessed held a TV, was nearby and on the opposite wall was a large fireplace with a fire already burning. The gleaming oak floor had a plush rug in the center of it. The festive fairy had been at work decorating in here as well. There was greenery along the mantle and groups of candles on tables. If she must be in this clinic, then she had won the lottery for the perfect room. She could hide out here in comfort.

"One of the staff should've put your luggage in here." He looked around. "There it is. Great." He pointed to the far side of the room where there was another door. "Through there is your bath. You'll find a hot tub, which I encourage you to use often. I'll leave you now to settle in. You don't have to be at dinner tonight. A tray of food will be sent up. Breakfast is between six and eight in the dining room. I'll let Flora know you've arrived. She may not have a chance to check in with you this evening, but you can expect to see her first thing in the morning. One of the staff will come and collect you at seven for breakfast. Is there anything you need before I go?"

Cass had slowly wandered around the room as he spoke. "I don't think so."

"If you have any questions, just pick up the phone. Somebody is on duty twenty-four hours a day. I hope your stay is a positive one."

Before he could say more a man appeared in the hallway behind him. "Lyle, you said to let you know when Andy Wallace arrived. The ambulance is at the back entrance. I'm on the way after the wheelchair now."

"Thanks Walter. I'll go down." Lyle turned to her. "See you around, Ms. Bellow."

Later that evening after dinner, Lyle bowed his head against the howling wind as he walked to his cottage. Seeing the once strong, always smiling Andy Wallace with sunken eyes and needing a wheelchair had made for a tough last few hours.

Andy was older than him. They had only been acquaintances growing up. Still, Lyle could remember Andy and Nick, Lyle's best friend Charles's older brother, laughing and always into something. Now Andy was a shell of that person. After an IED had exploded under his Humvee in Afghanistan he was a patient in a clinic started in honor of Nick. The irony was sickening.

Ms. Bellow wore the same sad expression as Andy. That look implied the weight of the world lay on her slender shoulders. His staff had their work cut out for them with those two. He and Charles, the Laird of Heatherglen and a doctor as well, had discussed both patients but Lyle suspected there was more to Cassandra Bellow than was on paper. She didn't even try to hide her desire to be elsewhere.

That resolute and dejected air about Cass indicated a serious psychological injury, but she carried her issues like a backpack they were so obvious. Maybe being at Heatherglen would help her with not only her physical problems but with what was bothering her heart and soul as well.

He recognized that look in both his residents because he'd seen it in his own eyes every time he'd shaved while serving in the Royal Army Medical Corps. All the men in his family had been expected to make a career in the armed forces and he hadn't disappointed. As one of his father's two sons, Lyle himself had been encouraged, then expected, to join the army. The importance of serving had been drummed into him his entire life. Yet medicine had pulled at him. To find a happy medium he'd combined the two.

Despite that compromise, he'd found the discipline and unwavering devotion of military life wasn't for him. He wanted to concentrate on caring for people in the way he loved best, personally. To his father's disappointment and ongoing puzzlement, Lyle had resigned his commission and returned home, remaining in the reserves.

His father still hadn't given up on the belief that Lyle would return to active duty someday soon. Every time they were together the subject came up. Now that his father's health was declining, the pressure had grown. If Lyle resumed active service, he could make his father's last few years happier, make him proud. But the exchange would be that Lyle would be miserable.

Charles had been in the process of setting up the clinic when Lyle had returned home from overseas. He'd asked Lyle if he would consider being the administrator, as well as run the emergency centre for the surrounding villages. Lyle had accepted and never looked back. He had found where he belonged. Still, his father's disappointment weighed on him.

The decision to return to the military hung there. Then there was his obligation to the clinic…

While he'd been in the Middle East that hopeless look he recognized in Cass's and Andy's eyes had grown in his own after receiving his "Dear John" letter from Freya. He had been caught in a net with no way out. Freya had called a halt to their relationship while he had been thousands of miles away, unable to talk to her face to face. For months the pain had been like a gnawing animal in his chest. It wasn't until he had returned and started work at the clinic that he could at last breathe and see the relationship for what it was.

Lyle continued along the snowy, muddy path toward his cottage. He knew this walk by heart. The moon was large tonight and he didn't need his torch. From experience he was sure his housekeeper had left a fire laid. The thought of lighting it and a warm drink kept him moving. Thankfully he had a full belly from the meal he'd shared with the residents before leaving the clinic. He wasn't required to dine at the castle, but Mrs. Renwick was a much better cook than he was. Since he didn't much enjoy eating alone, he ate most of his meals at the clinic. And just as he'd expected, the two newest residents hadn't been in attendance.

Going through some paperwork in his office the next morning, he allowed his thoughts to wander to Ms. Bellow. He had gone to Andy Wallace's room to make sure he was comfortable and had spoken to the overnight nursing staff about him. Yet despite his curiosity about Cass, Lyle hadn't searched her out. Because she wasn't under his direct care, he couldn't think of a reason to do so. Flora would have her case well in hand. Still, he felt compelled to see Cass.

She'd whetted his curiosity for some reason. Something about her sharp, self-assured tone and unwillingness to show her obvious pain made him want to understand what was going on behind those gloomy eyes. He'd felt her fragility when she had leaned against him. All bones and skin, as if she had lost weight. Being injured would have caused some of that but she was *too* thin. He felt the odd need to protect her, reassure her. Not that he would let that show. Still, just before lunch he couldn't stop himself from walking to the physical therapy department.

Lyle found Flora, with her dark head down, working at her desk. He knocked lightly on the door.

She looked up and smiled. "Hello, Lyle. What can I do for you?"

"I just wanted to check in on Cass Bellow. I haven't seen her today." He put his hands in his pockets.

"She was here for therapy this morning." Flora put down her pen. "She was ready to start when I arrived."

He leaned against the doorframe. "Great.

When we met yesterday, I was afraid she might be resistant."

Flora shook her head a little. "If there was a problem it was with her working too hard. She acted determined to be finished with her recovery well before the prescribed time. I had to remind her that she could hurt herself further if she pushed herself too hard."

"I'm sure that you'll see she takes it slowly and easily." Lyle took a step into the office. "By the way, did you tell her there's animal therapy as well? I got the impression it was a surprise to her when I mentioned it. I don't think she was told by her doctors in Germany that it's a central part of our program here."

Flora's eyes darkened with concern. "I did mention it but was called away before more was said."

"I'll speak to Esme. If Cass doesn't show up at the canine therapy center, then I'll talk to her."

Flora nodded. "Good."

"I told Cass the residents eat together, and she didn't look any happier about that."

Flora picked up the pen and tapped it on the desk once. "You and I have been at this long enough to know how to handle an uncooperative patient. We know physical issues often include adjusting to a new way of life." She lifted her shoulders and let them drop. "Why would Cass be any different?"

"Agreed. What about Andy Wallace? Have you had your session with him?"

"I'll see him this afternoon."

"Let me know how it goes. I don't think he's in any better frame of mind than Ms. Bellow."

Flora grinned. "We don't get all those great accolades for being the best therapy clinic for nothing."

"You have a point." He nodded his head at the door. "I'm on my way to get a sandwich for lunch. Care to join me?"

"Thanks, but I need to finish some paperwork for the boss."

Lyle chuckled. "And he appreciates your efforts. See you later." He left, walking to the dining room to pick up some food before returning to his office. Lyle planned to continue checking up on Cass and Andy for a few days until he was satisfied with their compliance, then he'd back away.

After lunch, Cass sat in her room by the fire, rubbing her thigh, glad therapy was over for the day. It had been grueling. Less from what she had been asked to do and more from her pushing herself. She had broken into a sweat and had clenched her teeth more than once not to cry out as pain had shot through her leg. Flora had warned her to slow down. It had been strenuous and stressful at best. Even her arm had resisted a couple of the exercises.

Making matters worse was the discovery Cass had made that she had stamina issues. The hospital stay in traction had taken a lot out of her. She'd always been fit, had worked out regularly with ease. Now she just felt frustrated. Regaining her strength wasn't going to happen fast enough.

That morning she'd been up and dressed by the time Melissa, a staff member, had knocked on her door. She had slept well the night before. Sleeping in the hospital hadn't been ideal. The peace and quiet of this country castle did have its appeal.

She had on some of the few clothes she habitually kept packed in her to-go bag. The knit sweatpants and T-shirt would have to do for workout clothes. When she and Rufus had caught the transport plane to Eastern Europe, nowhere in her plans had she thought to prepare for weeks of being in a hospital or being in a physical therapy clinic in Scotland in the winter.

Melissa had escorted Cass by elevator to the ground floor. There she had been led to the dining room.

"I'll return in a few minutes to show you to the physical therapy department," Melissa had said.

There hadn't been anyone else in the room. Cass had been thankful for that. She'd gone to the buffet and helped herself to a boiled egg and a slice of toast. She had just finished her second glass of orange juice when the woman returned.

"Flora's ready for you."

After placing her dishes on a tray, Cass followed Melissa down a long hall off the main one. They entered an area that looked like a gym where exercise equipment faced a bank of three large windows. In another corner of the spacious room were mats. Two high padded tables sat in the middle.

"You can have a seat on a table and I'll let Flora know you're here," she'd been told.

Cass scrambled up on the table with more effort than she liked.

A leggy, dark-haired woman wearing what looked like the latest fashion in exercise clothes soon joined her. Dressed in a hot pink jacket over a black top and leggings that came to mid-calf she made Cass feel extra-frumpy in her outfit. The woman even wore makeup.

She offered her hand, "Hi, I'm Flora Mc-Neith. It's nice to meet you, Cass. I apologize that I wasn't here to meet you yesterday. I'm sure Lyle took good care of you."

"Who? Oh, yeah, the doctor."

She chuckled. "Most woman consider him more memorable than that. We should get started on your therapy."

Over the next hour Cass showed Flora the range of motion in her leg and arm. For the first thirty minutes they concentrated on her leg and the last half-hour on her arm. Flora applied a cold compress before working with either part of her body, then a warm one after.

When they were through Flora said, "I'm sending you to the whirlpool for half an hour. After lunch someone will show you to your afternoon therapy at the canine therapy center."

She didn't give Cass time to respond before she turned to another patient who had entered the room. Cass had no intention of going to the canine therapy center. She wasn't ready to be involved with a dog again, any dog. Wasn't sure she'd ever be ready. Why had her doctors in Germany insisted on sending her to this clinic when they knew her background? Maybe they had thought it would be what she needed since she had been a dog handler, but she wasn't emotionally ready. She would just make it clear, without explanation, that she wouldn't be going to the canine therapy center.

As she walked toward the door marked "Whirlpool" Cass groaned. She almost cried with pleasure as she slipped into the hot swirling water. Today she had taken the first step towards her complete discharge and regaining her life. The one that didn't include Rufus.

After her trip to PT she'd stopped by the dining room long enough to grab a sandwich, leaving the soup behind. With food eaten, a warm shower taken and clean clothes on, Cass now had a nap on her agenda. She would be perfectly happy spending the rest of the day in her room.

She woke with a start when there was a sharp knock on her door. "Coming." Cass opened it to find a staff member there. This time it was a young man.

"I'm here to show you the way to the canine therapy center."

"I'm sorry but I don't feel like going." What she really meant was she *wasn't* going.

The man studied her a moment as if he expected her to say more, then nodded. "I understand."

Cass settled back in the chair and looked into the fire. She knew her abilities and strengths. The wound of losing Rufus was too raw. Her emotions in general were stretched to snapping point. She couldn't cope with the thought of interacting with a dog even if it was supposed to speed up her recovery.

She loved her job, but could she ever return to it, ever get so involved with another animal that she risked reliving this almost unbearable suffering? What if it wasn't a dog? Could she ever open up enough to anyone again to take the chance of losing her heart?

CHAPTER TWO

LYLE STOOD OUTSIDE Cass's door. She had refused to go to her canine therapy appointment. From the information he'd received from Flora she'd been more than game to do the work in physical therapy. Why was she balking at the rest of the program?

It was important. He and his colleagues had been highly successful in using canine therapy in the recovery of their patients. Cass needed to participate. He had read in her paperwork that she'd worked as a dog handler for search and rescue. Certainly she wasn't afraid of dogs. If anything, he would have thought that she would be eager to meet her assigned dog.

Lyle rapped on the door twice.

He heard a voice call, "Just a minute." Then a few seconds later the door opened.

Cass was dressed in a T-shirt, a zip-up hoodie, jeans and socked feet. She only came as high as his shoulders. She pushed at her short blonde hair, her tone demanding as she said, "Yes?"

"I understand that you don't want to go to your canine therapy appointment." Frustration with her resistance made him sound sterner than he'd intended.

"You understand correctly." She stepped back into the room.

He moved to just inside the doorway. "It's part of the program here. Everyone's required to participate."

"Why?" She stood feet slightly apart as if preparing for a fight.

He lowered his voice. "Because we've found that people recover faster when part of their therapy involves a dog. It's almost crucial to full recuperation. Why don't you let me show you the way to the center?"

"No, thank you." She put her hand on the door.

His brow rose. Did she intend to close it on him? "Are you in pain? Do I need to speak to Flora?"

A look of something close to panic filled her eyes. "No, I'm just tired. I don't feel like it today."

He checked his watch. It was too late now for her to go anyway. She had already wasted half her time. "Okay, that's understandable.

Rest is good. Take the remainder of the afternoon off. I'll see you at dinner."

She made no comment as she closed the door.

Lyle had to back out into the hall to avoid having the door shut in his face. When was the last time he'd been thrown out of a room? He couldn't even remember one. People didn't treat him like that, yet Cass had effectively done so. He shook his head. She would be a tough nut to crack.

It was almost dark when Lyle started for home. Cass hadn't been at dinner. Neither had she ordered a tray. He had left his meal long enough to go to her room, determined he'd be less understanding this time. If she couldn't follow the clinic protocols, she would be transferred elsewhere.

There was no answer when he knocked on her door. He tried three times before he called her name. Finally, he opened the door a crack and listened for the shower running. Nothing. He called again then stuck his head in to look. Cass wasn't there. First thing in the morning he was going to confront her when she showed up for her PT session with Flora.

A short time later Lyle turned to go through the gate leading to his cottage when he saw a dark shadow of a person down the way. They were sitting on the fence. Who was it? He was acquainted with most people around here but didn't recognize this person. The locals knew better than to sit outside at this time of year. His conscience wouldn't allow him to go home without first checking on the stranger.

He didn't wish to scare whoever it was, so he approached slowly. Still, there was no movement. Were they so deep in their thoughts they didn't hear him walking up? He stepped closer. He still couldn't tell if it was a man or a woman. The person didn't move. He went nearer, close enough he could touch them. Just as he was about to, they turned and looked at him. *Cass!* He had assumed she was safely in the castle somewhere, if not already back in her room. He would have never thought she might wander out into the night and cold. What had possessed her to come outside?

All she wore was a thin jacket. Her hands were shoved into her pockets. She wasn't dressed adequately for this weather. She should have on a woolly hat and scarf and a thicker jacket. "What're you doing here?"

She looked away, toward the last of the dying light.

"Are you okay? It's much too cold to be sitting here."

"I had to get out. I've been cooped up in a hospital for weeks. I needed some fresh air." Her words were so soft he leaned forward to hear them.

Lyle glanced in the direction she was looking and saw nothing that should hold her attention. He could only guess that her thoughts were so deep she had no idea what danger she was in. Could she even find her way back to the castle?

But first things first. "How long have you been out here?"

It took a moment before she answered, "I don't know."

Had frostbite started? He needed to get her out of the cold.

"Why're you here, Doctor?" Her voice sounded stronger.

That was encouraging. Much more like herself than her first few words. He pointed. "I live just down the lane there."

"Oh." Cass glanced over her shoulder then shrugged as if disinterested.

"I went to your room looking for you during dinner. I thought by now you would've come out of hiding and gone to your room for the night, prepared to ignore any knock on your door." He took a seat beside her.

This time she really looked at him. "What gave you that idea?"

"The expression on your face when I told you that you'd be expected for dinner in the dining room. I guessed you weren't planning to come. However, I didn't expect you to run outside to get away."

She pursed her lips and nodded. "Yeah, I don't think I'm gonna make those communal meals. And I'm not running away."

"We're not going to discuss that now. What we need to do is get you inside and warmed up." He stood.

Cass didn't move. Instead, her attention went to the sky once more. "Don't worry about me. I'm all right."

Lyle's brows drew together. He was sure she didn't appreciate the full effect of his reaction because of the dim lighting. "So you're knowledgeable enough about the area that you can get around without getting lost?"

Cass straightened and glared at him. "I work in search and rescue. I assure you I can manage to get myself back to the castle."

There was spunk in her voice. "That remains to be seen. You're obviously ignorant of the danger of being out in this weather without adequate clothing. I'm not taking any chances on losing one of our residents to exposure. Right now, you're going to the closest warm place and that's my cottage. When you're defrosted and dry, I'll walk you back to the castle."

It wasn't until that moment that Cass registered she was bone cold. How long had she been sitting here, staring off into space?

"Come with me. My cottage isn't far." He offered his large gloved hand, palm up.

She stared at it a moment. Was she acting crazy, like he already thought she was? Cass took his hand just long enough to slide off the wall. He turned and she trailed after him. They didn't go far before they entered a small clearing with a two-story stone cottage sitting in the middle. Trees surrounded it. A light over the door was on and another burned brightly in the window. Someone was expecting him.

"Is your wife going to mind you bringing a wayward patient home?"

"If I had one, she wouldn't mind." He walked to the door and opened it, then turned and waited for her to enter.

Cass stepped in, giving him room to follow. They stood in a small hallway. He waved a hand toward a room off to one side as he closed the door and began removing his coat. "Go on in and take off your shoes. They must be wet. I'll have the fire burning in a minute."

She entered what must be his living area. There was a small couch and a large leather chair situated close to the fireplace. The seat of the chair had a dip in it. It was obviously the doctor's favorite spot. A lamp and a stack of books sat on the floor beside it. A desk with papers strewn across it was against the wall with a window that faced the front lawn. Behind the desk stood a wooden chair. On the other side were shelves full of haphazardly placed books and a few framed pastoral scenes on the wall. The room had a very masculine feel to it. The man certainly owned his space. Cass found that comforting and reassuring in some odd way.

Lyle soon joined her, minus his outer clothing and shoes. He was in his socked feet, which made him seem even more approachable. "You don't have your shoes off yet? You need to get that jacket off as well. It looks like it's soaked through."

Cass started to remove a boot. "I can tell you spend a lot of time telling people what to do."

"You can thank my father and time in the army for that." He pulled a box of matches off the mantel, knelt and lit the fire. It soon came to life. "You really don't have any idea how long you've been outside?"

Cass considered pretending she hadn't heard

the question. She'd gotten lost in her thoughts, her disappointment and grief, but the last thing she wanted to do was confess why she'd been out there. "No, I'm not sure."

He stood. "You really are going to have to be more careful around here. It's easy to wander somewhere you shouldn't. With or without snow."

Although she hadn't yet gotten her boot off, Cass removed her coat. It was heavier than usual. He was right. She hadn't noticed how wet she had become.

The doctor reached for it and she allowed him to take it. Going to the desk, he hung it over the back of the chair, which he then pulled closer to the fire.

"Do you regularly bring patients home to sit by the fire?" She dropped one boot to the floor.

He grinned. It was a nice one. The kind that made her want to return it. "No. I'd have to say you're the first. But then I only do it for people sitting on my fence who are obviously about to freeze to death."

Shivering, Cass removed the other boot and let it drop beside the first one.

He pulled a colorful knit throw of orange, browns and tan off the back of the leather chair and draped it over her shoulders. She pulled the edges around her. Warmth filled her immediately. After letting it seep in, she removed her wet socks and spread them on the hearth. With a sigh, she stretched her ice-cold feet out toward the flames. Rubbing her stiff damaged leg, she got comfortable on the small sofa.

"I'll go and brew a pot for tea." Lyle started out of the room.

"The English and their tea," Cass murmured.

"I heard that. And I'm Scottish. Not English," he said with a clipped note.

Cass winced. She'd just been chastised. Her mother would be displeased with Cass for being rude, no matter what the circumstances.

He looked over his shoulder. "I forget you're American. Would you prefer coffee? I think I have some in the back of the pantry." He waited, an expectant look on his face.

She mustered a slight smile. "No, tea is fine. You've already gone to a lot of trouble for me."

"No trouble." He left the room.

While listening to him moving around in another part of the house, Cass laid her head back against the cushion of the sofa and gazed into the flames. The feeling was returning to her feet. She wiggled them. This was nice. The most peaceful she had felt in weeks.

Lyle returned with a small tray. On it were two steaming mugs, a milk jug and a sugar bowl. "Do you take yours with sugar and milk?"

"I don't know. My coffee I like with both."

"Then let's try it that way." The doctor mixed the ingredients in and handed her a mug.

She wrapped her hands around it, letting the heat seep into her icy fingers.

He sank into his chair with his mug in his hand. The chair fit him perfectly. "How're you feeling now?"

"Much better. I had no idea how cold and wet I was."

Leaning forward, he rested his elbows on his knees with the mug between his palms. "You really need thicker socks and boots. There's a good shop in the village for those."

"My sturdy boots were cut off and discarded when I was taken to the medical tent. I went straight from the tent to the hospital and from the hospital to here. When I can, I'll buy another pair. And maybe replace my cellphone." She had said more than she had intended.

His brows went up. "Medical tent? I had no idea. Do you mind telling me what happened?"

"It wasn't in my file?"

He pursed his lips and gave a noncommittal shake of his head. "Yes, but I'd like to hear it about it from you. I think you need to talk."

"Being a shrink again, Doc?"

"It's Lyle, and I was going more for being your friend." He leaned back, looking completely comfortable. "If you don't want to talk about it that's fine."

Now she was being put on the spot. If she didn't tell him something he would think she was a head case. "There's not much to tell. I was searching for a girl lost in the rubble of a building after a major explosion in Eastern Europe. It had been two days and there wasn't much hope. I found her alive but in the process a wall fell on me. So now you have it." Cass had been careful not to use the word *we*. She didn't want to talk about Rufus. She refused to break down in front of this stranger, no matter how nice he was.

"Wow, that's some story."

And he hadn't heard it all. Wouldn't ever as far as she was concerned. "Yeah, makes for a great party story."

He gave her a direct look. "I think it makes you a pretty impressive person. Your type of work can be both rewarding and very depressing."

He was right about that. His piercing empathy made her conscious of her vulnerability. She wasn't used to people seeing through what she said that clearly. The men she'd had relationships with certainly hadn't—including Jim, her latest disaster. Now she had scars on her body. How would men react to them?

Lyle put the mug down. "How're your hands and feet feeling now?"

Relieved he'd changed the subject, she answered, "Instead of being numb they feel like needles are being pushed into them."

"That's good. The feeling is returning."

Giving him a wry smile, she brought the mug to her lips again. The warmth flowed through her, matching the heat in the room. "So how come the administrator of the prestigious Heatherglen Castle Clinic is living way out here in the woods?"

Looking over the edge of the mug, he gave her an indulgent look. "In the daylight it's not that far out. This was the gamekeeper's cottage. When I returned from serving in the Middle East I needed a place to live. Turned out this came with the administrator's job."

"I don't see you as the military type." He didn't strike her as a squared shoulders, stand-at-attention kind of man. His smile was too quick, his manner too easygoing to fit into that strait-laced world.

"Aye. I was born and bred to it."

The words were flat, suggesting that hadn't been a completely good thing. There was more there but she didn't ask. It wasn't her business and she didn't like him prying into hers, so she wouldn't.

"You were overseas?"

"Aye, two tours in the Middle East."

"That couldn't have been much fun." She was sure that was an understatement.

A dark look came over his face. "It wasn't."

He must have seen stuff similar to what she had in her work. She would never have guessed they'd have anything in common. Cass didn't want to talk about the similarities in their backgrounds. Instead she would rather lock it away and not think about the past. Or the pain. "So you were raised around here?"

"Yes. In the village of Cluchlochry. My parents don't live far from here. Where're you from?"

His tone led her to believe he loved the area. "Indiana, but I live in Montana now."

He raised his eyebrows and nodded approvingly. "I've been there. Beautiful scenery."

"It is. That's my favorite thing about it. But even with all the snow, it's pretty around here as well."

"In the spring it's like living inside an emerald it's so green." Reverence made his Scottish accent more pronounced.

Did it do the same when he whispered in

a woman's ear when he desired her? Heaven help her! *That* wasn't a thought she should be having. Where had that idea come from? She swallowed hard and wiggled her toes. Surely it was the fire making her skin so hot.

"Let me have a look at those. I want to make sure you don't have the beginnings of frostbite." He went down on one knee in front of her.

"Look at what?" Her mind had been in a completely different place. "Oh, my feet. I don't think that's necessary."

He gave her an odd look then patted his thigh. "But I do. Put your foot up here."

With reluctance she did as he requested. Lyle's leg was firm beneath her bare sole, his corduroy pants soft.

He cradled her heel gently in the palm of his hand. All his touches were functional and professional, yet a streak of response zipped through her. She pulled back and sat straighter, watching the top of his head with its light, curly red hair. Were those coils as soft as they looked? She almost reached out a hand. Almost…

"Wiggle your toes for me."

Her head jerked up. It took her a long second to comply.

His fingers traveled over her toes. She pulled

back but he held her foot securely. He raised his head, a slight grin on his lips. "Ticklish." It was more a statement than question.

"A little." It sounded childish to admit.

Cass groaned inside.

"There's no sign of frostbite here. That's good." He placed that foot on the floor. "Let me see the other one."

Cass didn't even try to resist this time. He gave that foot the same attention as the other, but without tickling her. For some reason that disappointed her.

"Wiggle," he commanded.

She did.

"Good." He rose from the floor and moved to pick up one of her socks. "These are still damp. You really are going to have to get some thicker ones when you buy those boots if you plan to take walks. When the snow melts it can get very muddy. I'll get you some dry ones to wear back to the castle." He left the room.

It was past time for her to get back to the clinic but his place was so cozy, so comfortable. Too much Lyle's space. She shouldn't be having such a reaction to him. This wasn't the time to add more conflicting emotions to those she already had.

He soon returned and handed her a pair of thick, very masculine navy socks. She had no doubt these would keep her feet dry. He took his chair while she pulled them on. Immediately her feet were warmer."

"These feel great. Thank you. I'll have them laundered and returned as soon as possible."

He poked at the fire, making sure the screen was secure around it. "No hurry. I know where to find them if I need them."

Cass reached for her shoes. "I think it's time for me to be going. I've taken up enough of your evening."

Lyle didn't disagree with her. Instead he rose and went into the hallway. With her shoes now on, Cass reached for her damp coat.

"Wait. You need a dry coat as well." He had one in his hand, holding it open for her. She slipped her arms in and he settled the heavy jacket on her shoulders. There was that same smell she had caught when she'd first met him. The coat swallowed her whole but it was like being wrapped in his arms. Although that was an unsettling and unrealistic notion, it was nevertheless a reassuring one.

Lyle pulled on his own outdoor clothing while she waited. He studied her a moment. "You need a hat, scarf and some gloves as well." Disappearing upstairs, he returned with a handful of woolen items.

"I can't take these. Surely you need them." She offered them back to him.

He shook his head. "I have a drawer full. My mother knits these."

Cass ran her hand across them. The wool was so soft. "It feels wonderful."

"Try on the hat. It may not be tight enough, but it'll be better than nothing." He watched her expectantly.

Cass pulled the dark tan hat over her head, tucking in stray hair around her face. She still held the scarf. "I'll be all right without this."

"No, you won't." His stern look stopped her from further argument.

Cass wasn't used to having people tell her what to do. A bit irritated, she wrapped the scarf around her neck. It too smelled of pine and wood smoke, like him. Those scents would forever remind her of Lyle.

She forced that thought out of her head and focused on tucking the ends of the scarf inside her borrowed coat. "Your mother does a beautiful job."

"Thank you. What I can count on is that you'll stay warm in them. These gloves will be far too large but they will work for right now. You'll need to buy some of those as well. Now, come on, it's time we got you back to the castle."

She inhaled. There was that scent again. Yes, she needed to get out of here. Something about Lyle and his home made her wish for things better left alone.

CHAPTER THREE

LYLE OPENED THE door and the bitter cold embraced her. Cass pulled the scarf a little tighter around her neck, glad to have it. Lyle closed the door behind them, blocking out all but the porch light.

It was cold and darkness had taken over. As they walked further away from the house she could see the stars shining brightly. She paused in awe. It was beautiful.

Cass had been to many places in the world, but few compared to how amazing it was here with the moon and the stars…and the peace. In the distance there was a rise with what looked like the ruins of an old building on its crest. She pointed. "What's that place?"

"That's the old castle keep. The first laird of Heatherglen build it. It's a tumble of stones now but you can get a beautiful view of the valley, including the village, from up there. There's a path to it, but I don't recommend you go off on your own. The path can be a bit tricky in a number of places."

"Are you worried about me wandering away?"

He searched her face for a moment. "I'd like to hope not, but based on the facts I have so far, I feel like you might."

"I repeat, I was a member of a search and rescue team." One that was broken now. She no longer had a partner.

He pulled a flashlight out of his pocket and turned it on now that they were way from the cottage. "I understand that, but surely you've always had help."

She'd always had Rufus. Had relied on him to return them back home safely. Now she had no one. At this particular moment Lyle was fulfilling the role Rufus had had in her life. Still, she wasn't sure she could ever let herself truly rely or care for anybody, whether dog or human, ever again.

"Search and rescue is an interesting vocation. How did you get started in that?"

"When I was ten my younger brother got lost in the woods while my family was on a camping trip. He was gone almost twenty-four hours. My parents and I were terrified we would never see him again. The search and rescue people saved the day. Later on in college I realized I wanted to help people like my family had been helped." She paused. Why was she telling this virtual stranger all of this? What about Lyle had her talking so much?

He matched his pace to her slower one. "You and your kind are special people. I worked with a few of you while I was in the army. Did you do your training there?"

"No. I didn't start that until after college. While I was in school I worked at the vet clinic at the university. I was there most weekends as a volunteer. Some of the dogs were retired search dogs. After working with them I had no doubt what I should be doing."

"It sounds like an exciting way to make a living." He sounded truly impressed.

Sometimes it could be too exciting. She had no interest in reliving the last few months of her life. "It can be, but it also has its downsides. It's awful to see people desperately searching for loved ones or learn that a family member can't be saved."

"I know what you mean. War can do devastating things to a body. Trying to piece it back together can be the stuff of nightmares." His sincerity convinced Cass he understood all too well.

In spite of her determined efforts to conceal her private hell, she was feeling uncomfortably vulnerable yet again. "I'd rather not compare notes on what we've seen." Her last assignment was at the top of the list.

"You're right. Some things are better left in the past."

Cass couldn't agree more. She'd had enough issues generated in the recent past to last her a lifetime. She wobbled when she stepped into a snow-covered dip in the ground.

His hand nestled in her elbow. "How's that leg feeling?"

"Like a building fell on it and it had more PT than it liked."

"I bet it does. You're doing too much. A walk outside might have been over the top." He moved the torch so that it illuminated the snow in front of her.

"I'm handling it." She was, just barely though.

"I spoke to Flora and she said you might have overdone things today."

She pulled her arm from his hold. "Are you going around checking up on me?"

"That's part of my job." Nothing in Lyle's voice was apologetic.

Cass stepped as far away from him as the path would allow. "Well, I'll have you know I don't need a babysitter."

"I'll keep that in mind. I also understand

you're in a big hurry to leave us. You know, you can hurt people's feelings with that attitude."

When was the last time she had been teased? Her personality didn't make people do that often. "I'm not as interested in people's feelings as I am in getting my leg and arm well again. You do know I could've made it back by myself. All I had to do was come out the gate and follow the fence back."

"That may have been so, but I couldn't take the chance of you getting lost. It looks bad in the press for the clinic to lose a patient."

No matter how she tried to push him away, or how close she came to rudeness, he seemed to take it in stride. She had to appreciate his sense of humor and self-assurance. He had an ability to make her smile even when she didn't want to or feel like it.

A whimper from somewhere up ahead caught Cass's attention. Her senses went on full alert. She searched the ground for who or what was making the noise. Her reaction came from years of being vigilant at her job. Unable to see clearly in the small amount of light, she angled her head to listen. There it was again.

Lyle turned his flashlight toward a hedge nearby. The sound came again. It was animal, not human. This time Lyle stepped in the direction of it.

"Do you hear that?"

"Yes." She didn't move from her spot. The noises brought back painful memories. Like the ones Rufus had made just before he'd died.

"It's an animal in trouble." Lyle took small steps toward the shrubbery, making the light arc back and forth. The whimper came again, and he focused the beam in that spot. "It's a dog."

Cass's chest tightened. She couldn't deal with a dog right now. Even a stray.

"Hey, buddy, do you need some help?" Lyle asked in a tender, soothing tone. His shoulder moved as if he were reaching out a hand.

There was a growl.

Cass still remained rooted where she was. She couldn't make herself step forward.

"We can't leave it out here in the cold. It looks like it's starving." Lyle reached out his hand again.

Another growl.

Lyle spoke over his shoulder. "If I can get it to come to me I'll take it to the canine therapy center. Esme will check it out and see about it."

Cass forced herself to take a step closer. She looked over Lyle's back to where the light was directed. He reached forward once more.

The dog snarled, showing its teeth.

"It doesn't look like it's going to let me take it. I can't just leave it here. I'm afraid it'll freeze before morning."

Cass was shocked back to reality. The animal was so obviously undernourished. It shook in the cold. Its big brown eyes had a pitiful, fearful look. Cass's heart lurched. She had to do something. Everything in her that made her vulnerable to getting hurt again reached out to this pathetic animal. She didn't want to care but couldn't help herself.

Lyle didn't understand Cass's standoffishness. After all, she had worked with a dog. He glanced back at her. She just stood there, staring at him and the dog. "I don't recognize it as anybody's around here. I know them as well as I know their owners."

Finally, Cass blinked and stepped forward, but there was little enthusiasm on her face. "Let me see if I can help." She went down on her knees, paying no attention to the wetness that must be seeping into her jeans. Removing a glove, she reached out her hand, letting the small scruffy dog smell her.

The dog slowly extended its nose. It obviously liked Cass far better than him. It crawled out from under the hedge and came to Cass.

Just a puppy, it was small with muddy matted hair. One of its ears stood up while the other flopped. It had an oddly patterned coat, making it look of mixed breed. Cass lifted the dog to her chest.

Lyle stood. "It figures. I've always been far better with people than animals. It likes you."

Cass gave him a dry smile. When she struggled to stand he helped her.

"The canine therapy center is right down this way. Not far. Just behind the castle. It used to be the stables. It's just through the woods." He led them back to the path. "We'll take it there. Esme will see to it."

Cass didn't say anything as she came to stand beside him. As they walked she held the dog close but not overly so. Was she afraid of the dog? Or was there more going on? Lyle would have thought she'd be the first in on a rescue.

Soon they reached the center. The lights were still on. "Esme must be keeping another late night. I'm glad I didn't have to call and get her out in the weather again. She's the veterinarian. This therapy center/veterinary center is Esme's brainchild." He hurried ahead and held the door for Cass.

She moved in past him.

"Esme, it's Lyle," he called as the door closed behind him.

"Hey, be there in a sec," came Esme's voice from another room.

She soon appeared with a broad smile on her face. Her short blonde hair was disheveled, as if she had been running her hands through it. "What's going on?"

Lyle nodded toward Cass, who still held the dog. "We have a patient for you."

Esme looked at the dog then gave Cass a questioning look.

"Esme, this is Cass Bellow, one of our new residents. She hasn't made it down to meet the dogs yet, so you haven't met her."

"Welcome, Cass. So, who do you have there?" Esme reached for the dog.

It growled.

"Aw, I see you have that special touch," Esme said, speaking to Cass. "Bring it back here and I'll give it a look." Esme led them down a short hall into an examination room. "Put it on the table."

Cass did as she was told.

Esme went to touch the dog again and it rumbled a complaint deep in its chest.

"I'll give him something to ease his anxiety." Esme went to draw up a syringe of medicine.

"Apparently Cass has that special something

with animals." Lyle looked at her, expecting to see a positive expression, but instead she appeared distraught. What was wrong?

Esme quickly and efficiently gave the dog an injection. It soon rested easily in Cass's arms. "You can put him on the table now. He shouldn't be any trouble."

Cass placed the dog on the metal table and backed away. "I think you have this now." She looked at him. "I can find my way back to the castle from here."

Cass was out the door before Lyle could stop her.

"She seemed in a hurry," Esme murmured as she started examining the dog.

Lyle agreed. That accompanied intense curiosity about the stricken look on Cass face as she'd fled.

The next evening Lyle entered the dining room. A number of the residents were already there and engrossed in conversation. Cass wasn't one of them. He hadn't seen her since the night before. The few times he had left his office during the day she hadn't been anywhere in sight. After her reaction to the dog he'd been very interested in how she was doing.

Everyone was seated at the table and the

food was ready to serve when Cass entered the room. Relief washed through him. He had feared he was going to have to go and find her and he hadn't been looking forward to the conversation that would have taken place.

She was dressed in a simple white button-down shirt and jeans. On her feet were the same boots she'd worn the night before. Her hair was brushed back and it didn't look as if she had any makeup on. There was a fresh, simple air about Cass that appealed to him. Something he was completely unprepared for.

For too long he'd held onto Freya because she had been something safe and secure in a world he'd been unable to control. He had been too young, too unsure of life and couldn't see that before he'd gone overseas. Still, the way their relationship had ended had colored how he viewed potential partners. He was gun-shy, and he'd be the first to admit it. The next time he got involved with a woman he wanted it to be a mature, mutual lifelong commitment. That certainly couldn't be with a resident who would soon be gone and had her own life thousands of miles away. He needed to stop any kind of thoughts like the ones he was having now.

"We're glad to have you join us," he informed Cass as he stood and pulled out the chair next to him. Smiling, he added, "I was worried I might have to go out in the weather to hunt you down."

She gave the therapy dog belonging to the resident on the other side of her a long uncertain look before taking the offered seat. "It isn't because I didn't think about skipping out."

"I'm glad you changed your mind."

She gave him a direct look. "Hunger pangs changed it for me."

He nodded. "Whatever the reason, I'm glad you're here. Let me introduce you to everyone."

"You don't—" She didn't finish the sentence when those at the table turned to look at her.

"Everyone, this is Cass." Lyle then went round the table, giving each person's name. They either nodded or said hello to her as he went. She offered them all a tight smile.

The food was served family style out of large bowls and platters, passed around the table. Cass only took small amounts of a few items. At this rate she would never gain back the weight he suspected she had lost.

"I thought you might like to know that the puppy we found last night is doing well. Esme said he's fine except for being underweight. He should make a full recovery."

"That's good." She started picking at her meal. Cass wasn't helping much with making conversation. Lyle made another effort. "She's going to ask around and see if anyone claims him."

"That's nice." Cass took a bite of food as if she loathed doing it.

Roger, the man sitting on the other side of her, asked her a question. Cass gave him a two-word answer. Apparently, she didn't want to carry on a conversation with anyone. But she needed to. If he had ever seen someone badly in need of interaction, it was Cass.

He tried another approach. "I see the residents and staff have been busy in here today. It looks festive."

Cass looked around as if she was seeing the room for the first time.

How could she not react to the greenery and red bows hanging from the chandeliers, along with the large matching centerpiece of green boughs, velvet bows, and crimson balls? Or the mantel filled with decorations? In his experience it was the kind of stuff women loved.

Other than her hesitant look at the dog beside her, she appeared unaware of everything and everyone. He'd forced Cass into noticing him, but only for an all-too-brief moment. For some reason he wanted her to initiate an interaction with him. He wanted her to like him.

Lyle transferred his attention to Alice, who

sat on his other side. Maybe giving Cass space would help open her up a bit. He and Alice carried on a lively conversation about the upcoming village Christmas market beginning this weekend. They went on to discuss some of the other events planned for the festive season, like the annual Christmas festival at the castle, and the live nativity in the village.

"I was told there would be a tree lighting in the village and a parade in a few weeks." Alice's eyes lit up with excitement.

"There is and they even include some of the dogs from the center."

He glanced at Cass a few times during the discussion and caught her listening. When she saw him looking, she focused on her food again. He decided to try to draw her into conversation once more. "Cass, do you like craft markets?"

Her head jerked up. "I…uh… I do."

"Then you'll want to be sure and catch the minibus into Cluchlochry on Saturday morning. The village has a pretty impressive one. Great place to buy Christmas presents."

"I'll think about it." She pushed back her chair. "Right now I need to go for a walk before it gets dark."

"Hey, before you go could I speak to you for a moment in private?"

Her expression said no. Yet she answered, "Okay, but just for a minute. I really want to walk."

"I promise not to take up too much of your time." He rose when she did and followed her into the hall. "Why don't we go to the lounge?" With a hand he directed her down the hall. She headed that way and he joined her. They turned a corner and entered another hall. At the first doorway, Lyle opened the door to the large room with numerous sitting areas. A fire roared in the fireplace in the center of the main wall. Windows filled the opposite side.

"Why don't we have a seat?"

"I'm starting to feel like I'm being brought into the principal's office. You could have gotten on to me about not going to canine therapy again today in the hall outside the dining room." Cass sat on the edge of a cushion of the closest sofa.

"I could have, but I'm more interested in finding out why you're so resistant to the idea of canine therapy. Especially since I know your job entailed working closely with a dog. I assume you at least like animals a bit. I noticed you were slow to help with the dog we found and left the center as quickly as you could. I read in your file that you lost your partner." He didn't miss the stricken look that flickered in her eyes. "Is that what the problem is? I'd like to help. The staff here would like to help."

Cass shot to her feet. "I don't want your help or anyone else's. If you want me to go to canine therapy, fine. I'll be there tomorrow."

"There you are." Charles walking toward them stopped anything further Cass might have said.

Lyle came to his feet. "Hi, Charles. I'd like you to meet Cassandra Bellow. She's one of our newest residents. Cass, this is Dr. Charles Ross-Wylde. Also the Laird of Heatherglen and Esme's brother."

Charles smiled at Cass. "It's nice to meet you. Please call me Charles."

"Hello. You have a lovely home…castle." Cass's words were tight and formal. She glanced toward the door.

Charles chuckled. "Thank you. You're American, aren't you?"

"I am."

"You must be the woman who works in search and rescue?" He gave her an earnest look. "Interesting job."

"It can be." Cass looked toward the door again. "Why don't I let you two talk?" She slipped away.

Lyle watched her go. He had no doubt Cass would keep her word about going to therapy.

How much she would get out of it was another question. He'd just have to trust that the dog she was paired with would do what was needed to help her heal.

"Lyle."

He looked at Charles, who was grinning at him with twinkling eyes. "What?"

"You like her, don't you?"

"Why would you say that?" Lyle didn't want to discuss his confused reactions to Cass Bellow. Not even with his best friend Charles.

He laughed. "Because I called your name three times before you answered!"

Lyle wanted to groan. Now Charles would ask questions every time he saw him. "Did you have something important you wanted to talk to me about?"

Charles looked at him with a knowing smile on his lips. "It isn't as interesting as Ms. Bellow but we need to talk about Andy and his progress."

"Ah. Why don't we go to my office to do that?"

Cass was still stomping and swinging her arms in exasperation when she reached the main road after the long walk down the castle drive. How dared Lyle treat her as if she were a disobedient child? She was doing her physical therapy. Aware of what she needed, it wasn't canine therapy. But he wasn't going to give up.

She'd gone to dinner like he wanted, wasn't that enough? She would go to the canine therapy center tomorrow all right, but her participation in the therapy would be minimal and uncooperative. That should keep him off her case.

"Be strong," she said to the trees, and shoved her hands into her jacket pockets. When her brother had been lost, her mother and father had hugged her too tightly and had constantly reminded her they all had to remain strong. Afterwards Cass had used the mantra "Be strong" whenever she'd felt helpless. Even now, years later, she was using it to defy that feeling.

"Be strong!" she yelled to the sky.

She'd been strong when Jim had broken her heart, then soon after that when she'd learned that Rufus was gone. She'd been strong when the doctors had warned her she might never regain full use of her crushed arm and leg. She had been strong during the grueling hospital stay. During her agonizing physical therapy sessions here. Only it didn't matter how strong she was. Nothing changed. She was alone with no one to lean on.

The sound of a vehicle coming up the road drew her attention. The driver was going too fast for the icy conditions. As it came around the curve the back end went one way and then the other. The skid landed the front end of the car in the stone wall between Cass and the road.

She hurried out the castle gate and over to the car with her heart pounding, ignoring the ache in her leg. The engine was still running even though the hood was crumpled. The hot air of the radiator hitting the cold air created stream, making it difficult to see.

Cass reached out to touch the side of the car with a shaking hand. She'd not done any rescue work or even given anyone medical attention since her last assignment. Now here she was faced with an accident without the support of her partner. Could she do it? Would she break down and cry? She inhaled deeply, bracing herself. "Stay strong."

She ran her hand down the side of the car to keep her bearings as she worked her way to the driver's door. Cass pulled it open. She could, would, get through this.

The driver groaned, his palm pressed to his forehead.

"Are you okay?" Her instinct and training kicked in. "Don't move. You could have more injuries."

"I'm fine." His words were slurred.

She placed a hand on the man's shoulder. "I'm an EMT. I know what I'm talking about. More help will be here soon."

The man pulled his hand away from his head. Blood covered it.

"Don't move," she said firmly. "Keep your head back. I'm going to reach in and turn the engine off." She found the ignition key and turned it. The steam dissipated.

There was a moan from the back seat. She had someone else to check on. If she only had a cellphone to call for help. Hers had been damaged in her accident and she hadn't had time to replace it yet. Surely the driver had one. "Sir, do you have a phone? Tell me where it is, don't try to find it yourself."

The man gave her a weak yes and told her it was in his jacket pocket. Cass carefully reached inside his pocket and retrieved it.

Cass quickly dialed 999. When a person answered, Cass gave the call handler all the necessary information. She then stepped to the rear passenger door. Pulling it open, she found crumpled in the footwell a lady of around sixty. "You're going to be fine. I know you're in an uncomfortable position but try not to move."

The woman groaned, but Cass knew from the sound she was barely conscious. Using her fingers, Cass searched for a pulse in the woman's neck. She located one but it wasn't strong.

A voice she recognized as Lyle's said from behind her, "Don't move her. She may have concussion."

Cass said over her shoulder, "I've already told her that. And I've already called for help."

"I know. I must have called right after you."

She needed to get the man's bleeding under control. "Do you have any supplies?"

"No. I was on my way home when I heard the crash."

Cass stood. "You see about this woman and I'll look for a first-aid kit."

She worked her way to the front passenger door. Opening it, she searched the glove compartment for anything they could use. All she found was a stack of napkins. Those would have to do.

"Cass, we need to lay this lady down on the seat so I can examine her properly," Lyle said.

"Okay, take these napkins and have the man hold them to his head. I'll crawl in the back and help lift the woman up."

Lyle accepted the napkins and applied them to the man's head. "I need to get him to the clinic to stitch him up, but first we need to take care of this woman. She's lost consciousness."

Cass had been busy climbing into the backseat on her knees while he talked. Her leg rebelled at the position but she continued. She reached under the woman's arms and locked her hands across her chest. To Lyle she said, "Ready?"

"On three. One, two, three."

Cass pulled the woman against her chest. As the woman's back came up on the seat, Lyle grabbed her ankles and lifted. Soon they had her lying across the seat. She moaned and her eyelids flickered.

"Will you check her pulse and heart rate while I see if she has any internal injuries?" Lyle asked, as he started pressing on the woman's midsection.

"Her heart rate is steady but not very strong," Cass reported.

"Okay. So far I can't find any additional injuries." He continued to examine the woman.

A minibus pulled out of the castle gate and drew up alongside them.

"We need to get them both up to the clinic where I can give them a thorough evaluation." Lyle continued searching for problems.

Cass looked at the top of his head as he worked. "Shouldn't we wait on an ambulance?"

"That'll take too long. It has to come from Fort William. We're the emergency care for this area."

"Really?"

Now he met her look. "Rural area. That's how it is."

That made sense.

He was an impressive man to assume the responsibility for so many lives.

The staff member who had been driving the minibus joined them.

"Ron," Lyle said, "we need to get these people to the clinic ASAP. The man should be able to sit up front. We'll need the stretcher for the woman."

Ron nodded and headed back to the minibus.

Lyle backed out of the car. "Cass, would you please continue to monitor her while I have a look at the man?"

"Okay." Cass picked up the woman's wrist and placed two fingers on the inside. It took a second but she located a pulse. Still shallow but steady.

"I'm going to get this man into the minibus," Lyle called. "You good there?"

"Yes." Cass remained focused on the woman, trying not to think about her own recovering leg and arm as she began to worry about the injured woman being exposed to the cold. "Bring a blanket if you've got one."

"Will do." A few minutes later Lyle returned, pushing a gurney with Ron's help. "It's going to take all of us to get her loaded."

The two men positioned the gurney right outside the door.

Lyle handed her the blanket. Cass spread it over the woman. He tucked it around her legs. "Cass, if you'll support her head and shoulders while Ron and I get on either side of her and lift her out, I think we can make it work."

Cass wasn't looking forward to the pain she was sure would rocket through her leg and arm from the exertion. That didn't matter. Caring for the hurt woman was more important. Cass worked her hands under the woman's shoulder blades and supported her head with her upper arms. "Ready."

"Okay Ron. One, two, lift!"

Slowly the two men maneuvered the woman over the seat onto the gurney. Keeping the woman's upper body and neck as straight and stable as possible, Cass crawled across the seat and out the other door. By then electrifying pain was coursing through every nerve of her leg. Her arms and back were convulsing under the strain. When she tried to stand, her traumatized leg gave way. She grabbed the gurney. Though it wobbled on its wheels, she managed to balance on her other leg.

"Damn," Lyle swore as he reached for her.

"I can't believe I got so caught up in what was happening I forgot you were a recovering patient. Sit down." He guided her to a seat of the vehicle. Giving her a stern look, Lyle ordered, "Stay there while we get this lady loaded."

Cass hated to admit it but she was relieved to sit. Her eyes were watering from intense pain. As she took a moment, emotions swamped her. Her loss of direction, missing Rufus, the fog of her future all came down on her. Sorrow tightened her chest.

Lyle gave her a concerned look. For a second Cass feared he would question her but instead he said, "Ron, let's get this woman strapped down and loaded." Mere moments later he returned to her. "It's your turn."

Clenching her jaw, she stood. No matter how sick and unsure she felt inside, Cass refused to let it show, even if she had to struggle to do it. She feared Lyle was too perceptive and had already guessed. Cass said with more confidence than she felt, "I can walk."

"Maybe so, but you aren't going down on my watch." He wrapped an arm around her waist and guided her to the back of the vehicle.

Hot awareness of his strong sturdy body zipped through Cass as Lyle held her tight. Unable to stop herself, she leaned against him. After hesitating a moment, she rested her arm around his middle back and hobbled to the minibus. She couldn't ignore the sensations simmering in her core any more than she could ignore her agonizing leg.

Lyle held her steady until she reached for the frame of the door. Cass was climbing into the minibus when she was lifted off her feet and placed gently on the floor. She looked over her shoulder. "Thanks."

"No problem. Have a seat and move down." Lyle wasted no words. He was all business.

She did as she was told, scooting down to the end of the small bench seat. Lyle joined her. Their bodies touched all the way along one side. Strangely she wanted to rest her head against his shoulder but she resisted the urge. She refused to show any more weakness. What would Lyle think of her if she had given in to that impulse?

Ron close the doors. They were soon moving. Lyle's attention remained on the woman on the gurney, which was locked to the floor with straps. She still hadn't regained consciousness. Lyle took her pulse as they rode. He gave Cass a nod.

From what Lyle had said, Cass assumed that they were headed to the castle. By the winding of the road she could tell she was right. After making a big circle, Ron backed the minibus to a stop. Seconds later he opened the door.

Lyle climbed out with one agile move. "You stay put," he told her. "I don't want you to fall. Someone will be out to get you." He didn't wait for her response before he and Ron unhooked the gurney and rolled the woman inside.

Cass forced herself not to shake. Memories of lying in the rubble of that building flooded back. The sound of her calling Rufus's name and him not answering. The waiting until someone could get to her. Panic rose when Lyle didn't come. Pain throbbed through her body. She needed to get out of here.

She searched the area she could see. It was a part of the castle she wasn't familiar with. The vehicle was backed up to a small loading dock with two double doors. Her impatience grew to be an almost living thing. She had to do something. What if Lyle needed her help? Just as she was about to rise, Ron came through the doors, leaving them swinging. He gave her a glance then hurried down the steps nearby. Her heart dipped. He must be going after the man up front.

With Ron and Lyle concentrating their energies on the injured people, it would be some time before someone would come to assist her.

She decided she wasn't in so much pain that she couldn't get herself inside.

Giving her leg a rub, she pushed up off the bench, making sure she didn't use her right arm. It took effort. With a tight jaw she made it to her feet. She slowly moved out of the minibus, steadying herself by pressing her hand on the side of it. Just as she was stepping off, the doors swung open again and out came Melissa, pushing a wheelchair.

She positioned the wheelchair just outside the van doors and stepped inside. "Lyle sent me out for you. He said you wouldn't stay seated long. I guess he was right."

Cass didn't like Lyle thinking he knew her that well, but she couldn't deny he was right. She took a step forward, trying to keep as much weight as possible off the leg. Cass couldn't deny the wheelchair was welcome.

"Here, let me help." Melissa supported Cass to the chair and assisted her into it.

With Cass secure, she pushed her inside. They entered a large emergency examination room complete with all the most up-to-date equipment. Cass was fascinated. She'd had no idea this area of the clinic existed. There were many facets to Dr. Sinclair and his "clinic".

Lyle stood beside the older lady, who still lay on the gurney. Thankfully she was now conscious and talking to him. Ron was busy cleaning the driver's head wound at an exam table nearby.

"What can I do to help?" Cass asked, putting her hands on the arm of the wheelchair, preparing to stand.

Lyle gave her a piercing look of reprimand. "Nothing. You've done enough. You need to take care of yourself."

"Surely you need some help." Cass looked from him to the man Ron was seeing to and back.

Another member of the nursing staff rushed in. Behind her came another.

"We have plenty of help. Melissa, please see that Cass gets to her room. I'll let Flora know what's happened. She may want to examine you. Melissa, Cass actually might also benefit from some time in the hot tub." Lyle's attention returned to his patient.

Seconds later Cass was being wheeled out of the room. It didn't take Melissa long to get her up to her room and hot water running in the tub. Cass gratefully slipped into the whirling water, looking forward to the relief it would bring her leg and arm. She'd survived her first emergency without Rufus. It had been a sad moment but somehow an encouraging one. In a small way, Cass was moving forward.

* * *

Lyle was ready for some rest but he needed to check on Cass first. The ambulance from Fort William had arrived to take the injured woman to the hospital. Lyle had stitched the gash on the man's forehead and sent him home with family members. After a quick check on Cass he was headed for his cottage and bed. The adrenalin spike of handling an emergency had worn him out.

He knocked lightly on Cass's door in case she was already sleeping. After waiting a minute and getting no answer, he turned to leave. He would see her tomorrow.

The door opened a crack. "Yes?"

He could only see a sliver of her but it was enough to tell that her hair had been pushed back and her face was freshly scrubbed. She looked adorable and unsure at the same time.

What was it about her that captivated him? That pulled at him like no other woman he knew did. Was it her strength? Determination? Her vulnerability? He needed to solve the puzzle and move on. Cass wouldn't be here long and he wasn't going to waste his emotions on anyone he didn't intend to keep forever. He'd already gone down that road.

The dirty street behind him was graveled with disappointment and heartache. He had vowed the lane ahead would be paved with the love and loyalty of a woman who wanted him as much as he did her. A lifelong partner. The next time he fell in love, he would get it right.

He shoved that fantasy aside and concentrated on what he was there for. "How're you doing?"

"Better after a hot bath."

"Good. You were impressive out there, Cass. You stayed in control. I know you must have been in pain. You should have said something. More than that, I should've thought." Guilt filled him. "I'm sorry."

She opened the door wider. "Hey, I'm an EMT. I'm trained to help."

"True, but you're also a patient here. I should have remembered that." She looked cute in her T-shirt with her pink-tipped toes.

"I'm fine." For once her eyes weren't clouded with hidden feelings. In fact, there was a hint of a smile in them.

"I'm glad. Then I'll let you get some rest." He needed to go. Right now. He started down the hall.

"Hey, Lyle."

He almost kept going, but curiosity got the better of him.

"You were pretty impressive out there too."

He smiled. It felt good to have someone

praise him, especially Cass. He was confident in his abilities, but it didn't hurt to have others notice. His father certainly hadn't. "Thanks. Sleep well, Cass."

CHAPTER FOUR

CASS'S HAND SHOOK as she wrapped it around the handle of the glass door of the canine therapy center the next afternoon. She had said she'd keep her appointment and she would. But she wasn't looking forward to it.

The thought of having anything to do with a dog made her want to break down and cry. The pain of losing Rufus was still too raw. It might be silly for a grown professional woman to feel this way, but she didn't care. Rufus was gone. Some part of her clung to the irrational hope he would be waiting with his tail wagging when she returned home. No other dog could replace him.

She would do what she had to, then hurry to her room for a good cry.

When she jerked the door open the young man sitting behind the desk started. This was the same high-ceilinged room with the rough board walls where she and Lyle had brought the puppy a couple of nights before. He'd said it used to be the stables and she could now see that. The other night all that'd filled her mind was that she had a dog in her arms.

"Can I help you?" the man at the desk asked.

"I'm Cass Bellow. I'm a resident at the clinic."

He looked down as if checking a list, then back at her. "Oh, yes, we've been expecting you." As he got to his feet he added, "Come with me. Margaret assists with the canine therapy program. She's back here."

Cass forced her feet to move and followed him down a hall. It wasn't the same one Lyle and Esme had led her down to the examination room the other night. The man pushed through a swing door. Cass entered a room furnished with easy chairs.

A dark-haired woman was down on her heels next to a woman seated in an easy chair holding a small black dog of no pedigree. Cass recognized the woman in the chair from the dinner table at the clinic. Lyle had introduced them, but Cass didn't remember her name. Shame pricked her. She hadn't even tried.

"Margaret, this is Cass Bellow," the man announced.

The dark-haired woman looked at them, stood and came toward Cass with one hand outstretched. She smiled. "It's great to finally meet you."

Was that her subtle way of reprimanding her for not showing up for her earlier appointments? The temptation to run grew.

"I help Esme with the canine therapy here at Heatherglen," Margaret continued.

The man quietly left the way they had come in.

Staring at the small dog that was enjoying the woman's gentle pats, Cass's chest tightened. She wasn't ready for this. She had no interest in doing *anything* with a dog.

Margaret was saying, "I thought you might like to meet Muffin. He's a sweet little dog. He'll be your companion during your stay. Let me get him and you can get acquainted." She stepped through a side door.

Cass stood, knees shaking, in the middle of the room, looking everywhere but at the other woman. She didn't want any responsibility for a dog for the next month. Especially one named Muffin. Her breathing became shallow. Her mouth turned dry. She shifted from one foot to the other. The need to leave intensified. This was too much. A meltdown was building if she didn't get out of there. She wasn't ready, might not ever be. What if she became too attached to the ridiculous Muffin? She would be leaving soon. All this pain would be there again.

Without thought Cass bolted for the door and up the hall to the front room. She had to get out of there. Ignoring the man behind the desk calling her name, she shoved the door open and stumbled into the cold air. Sucking in a deep breath, she kept going, heading toward the castle. By way of a side door she'd found yesterday, she slipped inside unnoticed.

Instead of going to her room, where someone would surely look for her, she headed for the conservatory. While exploring she'd also found an alcove hidden behind some large palm plants and banana trees with only a small sofa. There she could lick her wounds in private.

Relief washed through her when she found the floral fabric-covered settee empty. She sat, pulling her legs up under her and wrapping the coat Lyle had loaned her tighter. When would the pain go away?

She had no idea how long she had been sitting there staring off into space when she heard, "Cass?"

Lyle.

She stiffened. How had he found her? It didn't matter. She had no intention of explaining herself. Why couldn't he just leave her alone? "Go away."

He just stood there.

Finally, she murmured, "How did you know where to find me?"

"I saw you come in here. When I had a call from the center I knew where to look."

Great. She'd believed she'd made her escape. Her focus remained on the green spots showing in the snow that was melting outside. "So now you're riding to the rescue."

Lyle came to sit beside her. "I'd just like to help. Be a friend. I was told you looked upset."

Maybe if she ignored him he would go away. Instead of him taking the hint to leave, he settled further back into the cushions, his big body almost touching hers. They remained like that for a while, neither saying anything.

"You're not leaving, are you?" Cass stared at the dust motes dancing in the sunbeam streaming through the glass.

"Not until I know you're okay." He stretched his legs out and crossed his ankles.

She huffed. "Let me assure you I'm not going to harm myself."

"I didn't think that but it's good to hear."

He settled back as though he was content to stay the rest of the day. As the silence between them grew so did her temper. She hissed, "What do I have to say to get you to leave?"

For a moment she thought he was ignoring her. When he did reply, concern laced his voice. "I'd like to understand why you're determined to have no part in our canine therapy program, especially since you work with a dog all the time."

Could she tell him? Would he understand? Was that the only way to get him to leave her alone? If he knew, maybe he would see to it she didn't have to go to canine therapy.

She opened her mouth to tell him about Rufus but the words stuck in her throat. If she said it out loud, then it would make it true. She didn't want that. Couldn't live with that. She closed her eyes tight. Maybe if she said it really fast she could get it out. "Rufus, my partner, died. Now I don't know if I can be around a dog all the time."

The moisture she had been banking for days seeped out of her closed eyelids. She took a deep breath in an effort to stop the sob welling in her throat but it didn't work. Instead she doubled over in agony. As she tried to catch her breath Lyle ran his large hand across her back in a comforting stroke.

Then he cupped her shoulder and pulled her against his chest. She buried her face in his shirt, her fingers clutching his sides. All the emotions she had held in check since the day that wall had collapsed flowed freely. The pain deep within her consumed her. Rufus was gone. Life as she'd known it had gone with him.

Lyle held her close, rubbing her shoulders and back. "Let it all out," he whispered.

Cass did. All the raw feelings she'd held in check for weeks flowed, leaving her nothing but a heaving shell. She couldn't stop the pain, fear and sorrow from escaping.

Lyle continued holding her and murmuring soft reassuring words while she clung to him.

She had no idea how much time had passed when she woke with a start. Disorientated, she still had a sense of safety. Slowly it dawned on her she was still in Lyle's arms.

Embarrassment flooded her. Placing her palms on his chest, she pushed into a sitting position. Yet one of his hands remained on her back.

"I'm so sorry for that ugly scene," she heard herself saying. "I don't know why I fell apart like that. It isn't like me."

"I'd imagine it was because you needed to. You've been under a tremendous strain." He shifted, putting his hands on his thighs.

She missed the reassuring weight immediately. Lyle was right, there was a lot of stress and emotion involved in her profession. She should be able to handle it. But where Rufus was concerned she was lost. Cass wiped at his sweater. "I've made a mess of your clothes."

"I don't mind. I'm glad I was here to help." He sounded as if he meant it.

"So part of your job description is to have patients cry all over you?" Cass managed a weak smile.

He looked at her tenderly. "Not all patients. I have to say you're a special case."

Warmth gradually replaced the coldness running through her. Lyle was a nice man saying all the right things. For an instant she wished he wasn't a doctor speaking to a patient.

"I knew about you losing your dog, it was in your file. But I had no idea that going to canine therapy would be so difficult for you. You've had a tough time physically and…" he paused "…emotionally. Flora, Esme and I didn't recognize that. I'm sorry. Would you like to talk about what happened? I'm a good listener." His words were encouraging, not demanding.

Cass shook her head, both in response and to clear it.

He waited a few moments then asked, "When did you learn the details of what happened?"

"I realized the wall was falling but I had no idea…" She swallowed. Her throat was tight and dry. Inhaling, she fought through the final pang of denial. "I didn't find out Rufus didn't make it until I woke up in the hospital. When I asked about him, one of the nurses had to ask around for the information."

Lyle put his arm around her shoulders again and gave her a supportive squeeze. "I'm sorry. It shouldn't have happened like that."

Cass continued to look at the windowsill. It was such a large one. Almost big enough to use as a seat. "No matter when I was told, or how, it wouldn't have made…the terrible truth any easier to hear."

"Maybe not, but at the very least the news should have been given to you in a sensitive manner." He sounded irritated on her behalf. "Will you tell me about your dog?"

She didn't want to, but he deserved to know why she'd just sobbed herself into an exhausted sleep all over him. "Rufus was more than my dog. He was my partner and best friend."

And her longest relationship. He been there more than once when a relationship with a man had ended. Those guys had either been intimidated by a woman who handled such an emotionally demanding job, or they didn't like her leaving for weeks at a time on the spur of the moment. For a couple of them her relationship with Rufus had been a bone of contention. They'd wanted all her attention and hadn't understood the uncanny connection between her and her canine partner. Now she had physical scars that they might find offensive, too.

Jim, the latest and the man she'd believed was The One, had felt her job was too risky. It had been nice to have someone worry over her at first, but it had soon started to feel restrictive. Despite their breakup he'd been kind enough to call her while she'd been in the hospital, but it had soon turned into a conversation that was more about him telling her *I told you so* than about his real concern for her. There had been no sympathy on his part for Rufus. She'd thought at one time they might have a chance at a real life together. Sadly, she'd really cared for Jim but there was no hope of that after their conversation.

Lyle removed his arm. She wanted it back. It was comforting. "How long was this dog your partner?"

"Four years. He was two when I got him. We spent the first eight weeks in training. He was born in Germany. Most good rescue dogs are. The Germans are known for breeding them to be work dogs. In fact, most of his commands

I gave in German." It felt better, and was easier, to talk about Rufus than she'd imagined.

"Interesting." Lyle waited.

She looked at him. His expectant expression suggested he was truly interested in what she was saying. Yet she couldn't imagine him actually caring.

"How did you train together?"

"Are you really interested?" What if he was just asking to keep her talking as part of her "therapy"? None of the men she had known before him had cared one way or another. Why would he be any different?

"Aye. I wouldn't have asked if I wasn't." His voice carried concern. It had been so long since she'd heard that in a man's voice, it struck a deep chord within her.

"I had to do a written test and have a physical. Then I had to have a home visit so the powers-that-be knew I could care for a working dog. An animal like Rufus can cost as much as ten thousand American dollars so handlers are vetted closely. That kind of money can't be wasted. Rufus had to have a physical as well, and learn obedience basics and detection, especially body odor recognition. It was pretty intense for both of us."

"A powerful bonding experience for you both."

Cass's chest tightened from the memories. They had indeed bonded. She had loved the dog, heart and soul. At least Lyle *seemed* to understand. "Though he was only four, he was getting old for a working dog. Rufus was going to have to retire soon. I had already put in the paperwork to take him after he was done."

"Going to canine therapy was almost like punishment for you. You should have said something." His distress was evident in his voice.

She looked away in horror. "And embarrass myself, like I did a few minutes ago?"

Lyle took hold of her hand. His was large, secure…comforting. "You haven't embarrassed yourself. It's okay to be human."

"Yeah, but blubbering all over you is a bit too human."

He leaned closer until his shoulder touched hers. "I didn't mind. I'm just sorry I kept pushing you into canine therapy."

"I figured you'd seen it in my file." She winced at how pitiful she sounded.

"Yeah, but that didn't mean I understood how close you were."

Great. He probably thought she had really gone off her rocker. "I don't know if I can handle being around a dog right now. I'll be leaving here in a few weeks and I, uh, just can't risk becoming attached to another one." What she wasn't telling him about was the heavy guilt she carried over the fact that Rufus had sacrificed himself to save her life. If he hadn't barked, she would have never looked up to see the wall starting to fall. Or that he'd jumped and pushed her out of the way. It had been a split second between her life and Rufus's death.

"I understand completely," Lyle said sincerely. "Would you consider an alternative kind of therapy, if we can come up with one? Maybe just helping out at the canine clinic. Not having a specific dog assigned to you."

She was doubtful it would work but she could try. At least he was trying to work with her. Somehow she had to get past this grief, rebuild her life emotionally and move on. Yet her heart protested with a fresh pang even as she said with caution, "That might work."

"If it doesn't, then we'll try something else." His sincere tone and expression convinced her he would at least listen if she complained. Lyle's comfort was the first she'd had since Rufus had died. She was going to hang onto it.

He let her hand go and shifted away. "Do you feel up to a bite to eat?"

"I don't want to go to the dining room."

"It's too late for that." He tilted his head toward the glass.

Cass was shocked to find it was dark. How long had they been sitting there? "I'm so sorry. I made you miss dinner."

"Not a problem. Mrs. Renwick will have left me something in the kitchen. Let's go see what we can find."

"I think I'll just go up to my room." She wanted to get away. Regain her composure.

"Nonsense. You must be hungry, and I could use the company while I eat."

She had kept Lyle from his hot meal. She owed him. "Okay, I can do that."

"Not the most excited acceptance I've been given to a dinner invitation, but I'll take it." He stood.

Cass liked his sense of humor. He seemed to take life as it came without too much angst. She lacked that ability. Her way of meeting life's challenges now consisted of worry, fear of failure and the guilty conviction she hadn't done enough to make a difference. She wanted to save everyone, give them what her family had received. The chances of achieving that desire were slim to none, but still it was her goal. Now she was just a mass of nerves, help to no one. Not even herself. Squaring her shoulders, she said, "I'll try to do better in the future."

He offered his hand. "That's what I like to hear. That old tough Cass. You had me worried there for a while."

Lyle still thought she was tough? She would have thought he would have seen her as the opposite after the last few hours. She took his hand just long enough to get to her feet. "How's that?"

He put his hands in his pockets and rocked back on his heels. "I don't handle crying females well."

"I'm sorry I made you uncomfortable." She couldn't meet his eyes.

"Hey, I'm glad I was here to help. Now, let's go and get some dinner." He started toward the hall and she joined him.

Lyle led the way to the kitchen. His heart went out to Cass. She was distraught over the loss of her dog. He knew well the empty hole loss could leave in your life. He had felt it intensely when Freya had left him. When he'd told Cass that he didn't handle women crying well, he hadn't been kidding. All he'd done was hold her.

The fact that he'd liked having her cry on his shoulder was a bit unnerving. What had begun as a professional obligation to check on a resident in crisis had ended in a very personal act of compassionate empathy. Was he drawn to her because he could sense her private suffering? Whatever it was, Cass held some sort of spell over him. One he didn't mind being captivated by.

Cass followed him quietly to the kitchen, seeming fine with doing so. They walked through the now silent dining room to the swing door beside the fireplace. He held it open for her as they entered the large commercial-style kitchen.

"Have a seat at the table." There was a small wooden one next to two corner windows in the large room. "I'll see what I can find in the fridge."

Her chair scraped over the tile floor as she took a seat.

Opening one of the doors of the very large fridge, Lyle announced with deliberate cheer, "Ah, we have roast beef and vegetable soup. How does a sandwich and a bowl of hot soup sound?"

"That's fine."

He glanced over his shoulder. "Again, I was looking for a little more enthusiasm."

A fake smile contorted her lips as she swung a fist overhead. "Great!"

He grinned. "That's more like it."

"Can I help?"

"Sure." He started pulling bowls and a platter off the shelves. When Cass reached him he handed her a few of them. She carried them to the table. Lyle followed with the rest. "You unwrap the containers while I get plates and things together." He searched cabinets and drawers for what they needed, making a couple of trips to the table to put everything down. She was halfway through removing the plastic wrap from the bowls when he said, "Now I'll warm up the soup if you'll make the sandwiches."

"All right."

He pushed the uncut loaf towards her. "I'd like two thick slices."

"Noted." She picked up a bread knife and start cutting.

Lyle ladled soup from its storage container into a saucepan and turned on the stove. As he stirred, he watched Cass work.

Standing, she placed two slices of bread on a plate and buttered them. That done, she unwrapped the rest of the containers. Next she cut slices of roast beef, laying them on the bread. She finished with condiments and lettuce.

Cass's movements were concise and efficient. She had a no-nonsense way about her. Her blonde hair swung over her cheek and she pushed it back with impatience as if she had no time for things to get in her way. She cleaned up as she went. He got the distinct impression she took responsibility for herself and expected others to do the same for themselves. It must have been a rare event for her to let someone witness her raw emotions. Strangely, he was honored he had been the one there for her.

Lyle carried the steaming saucepan to the table and poured the soup into the bowls he'd found earlier, then returned the pan to the stove.

As he came to take his seat at the table Cass inhaled deeply. "That smells wonderful."

He grinned. "I can take credit for it being hot but not for how it smells."

She returned his smile and his heart made an extra thump. He filled the two tall glasses with milk. "Those sandwiches look good."

"I can take credit for how they look but not how they taste." Cass was trying to mimic his accent.

They both laughed as they settled onto their chairs.

She gave him a shy glance. "I don't do Scottish well, do I?"

"I'm going with it needs work." He looked at her over his sandwich just before he took a large bite. He appreciated the sparkle in her eyes that had replaced the earlier dull sadness.

They ate in silence for a few minutes before Cass let her spoon rest against the side of the bowl. "Do you know how the woman we helped is doing?"

He nodded. "I spoke to her doctor this morning. They kept her in overnight for observation, but she seems to be fine."

Cass lifted a spoonful of soup to her mouth. "I'm glad to hear it. How about the man?"

"He'll come in next week to have his stitches removed." Lyle took another bite of his sandwich.

"You really are a jack-of-all-trades, aren't you?" She appeared fascinated.

He rather liked that idea. In fact, he liked her. It had been too long since he'd let himself be drawn to a woman. It would be short-lived, of course, as Cass would be returning to the States soon, but why couldn't he enjoy her company while she was here? It would certainly make his Christmas more interesting. "I wouldn't exactly say that I'm Santa, spreading cheer, but I try to help out where I can."

They finished eating and Lyle started cleaning the table. "Even with my special powers I'd better do the washing-up if I don't want to get on the wrong side of Ms. Renwick."

"I'll help," Cass said in such a firm tone he didn't dare argue.

Together they covered the food and returned it to the refrigerator. His hand brushed hers as she handed him a bowl and he saw color bloom in her cheeks. Despite her tough exterior, her face couldn't conceal her attraction to him. Her gaze met his before she quickly returned to the table to pick up their plates.

Instead of joining him again, she went to the sink and turned on the water. Now she was trying to hide from him. With that in mind, he did his best as he finished clearing away to give Cass space while she washed up. He was aware enough of her to realize she was trying to avoid more contact between them. Was she attracted to him? Was she noticing his every move, as he did hers?

Cass turned toward him, her hip resting against the counter. "Didn't you say that Ms. Renwick leaves food for you?"

"She does, but that doesn't mean she isn't particular about how her kitchen is kept." Lyle stacked the bowls in the cabinet.

"So, if I'm not careful I'll end up on her wrong side?" Cass hung a dishcloth back just as it had been when they'd come into the kitchen.

"I wouldn't worry about it too much, she's really a softy at heart."

Despite his assurance, they stood at the door

and gave the kitchen one last look before they exited the room.

"I don't think we've left anything out of place," Cass said as the door swung closed behind them. "My mother is just as particular about her kitchen."

"I'm sure Ms. Renwick will be pleased." That was the first time she'd revealed a personal detail without being asked. He was delighted she had begun to open up.

Cass led the way through the dining room and continued into the hall, where she stopped and turned. Her eyes flickered up to meet his gaze then down to the floor just as quickly. "Thanks for supper…and for, you know…" she glanced up at him in a self-conscious manner "…a while ago. My…uh, meltdown."

She looked so apologetic he crammed his hands into his pockets to keep himself from hugging her. "Not a problem."

"I'll give the canine therapy another try." There was determination in her words.

"And I'll speak to Flora and Margaret and see if they can work something out so you won't have to work with one particular dog."

Cass gave him an earnest look. "I'll do what I can to make that work. I really do appreciate you letting me cry on your shoulder."

To his complete astonishment, Cass placed a

hand on his shoulder, came up on her toes and gave him a quick kiss on the cheek.

Pleasure zipped through him. When he saw Cass's shocked face seconds later with its charming pink cheeks he was mesmerized. This tough woman appeared flustered. Her eyes had gone wide in surprise before she blinked a couple of times and looked away. She shook slightly and he feared she might fall. Lyle reached for her.

Cass stood close enough that he could smell the fresh scent of her hair.

"I'm sorry," Cass murmured.

Lyle lowered his head to hear her words, bringing his lips closer to hers. He watched them, the soft full pads that looked so delicious.

"That was inappropriate. I shouldn't have done that." Cass glanced at him then away.

"I'm not," he said quietly. "I rather liked it."

Her eyelids fluttered closed, then her gaze met his. They stood there watching each other for precious moments. The tip of her tongue made a flicker of an appearance. Lyle wanted a taste, just a small one, of that glossy moistness on her bottom lip. He lowered his head and placed his mouth over hers. Cass remained still in his hands. Lyle took the kiss deeper.

Cass returned it for a second before she

slipped out of his hands and whispered, "Good-night."

Lyle watched her walk away. Disappointment filled him. Everything in him wished he could stop her without frightening her. He wanted more than a chaste meeting of lips. It hadn't been nearly enough. He sought a full, no-holding-back kiss from Cass. There was an attraction between them he wanted to explore. It had been a long time since he'd experienced such a driving need to kiss a woman breathless.

CHAPTER FIVE

Cᴀss ᴡᴀʟᴋᴇᴅ ᴛᴏ the canine center the next afternoon still astounded she had foolishly kissed
Lyle. Making her embarrassment worse and
her pleasure more, Lyle had actually looked
pleased she had kissed him.

But she didn't do that sort of impulsive
thing. Ever. She thought through her actions
first. Never had she fallen apart like that in
front of anyone. To do something so rash only
showed how open the wound was that made up
her life. Then there had been her crying jag.
Until last night she had held it together despite
all she'd been through. Talking about Rufus
had broken her.

Lyle had been incredibly kind when she'd
really needed someone. Beneath his attention
she'd opened up like never before. He'd listened without judgement instead of running
away. Lyle acted as if he cared, understood
her loss.

Cass shook off that admission.

She'd kissed Lyle. What had she been think-ing? She hadn't been, instead she had just re-acted. It had been a stupid, careless move. Being here at the castle was about therapy and making a full recovery, not romance. Her heart couldn't handle those emotions right now. Even if it could, what did she imagine would come of it? Nothing, that was all that could happen.

As she entered the canine therapy center, Margaret greeted her at the door as if she had been waiting for her. Instead of taking her into the room where she had been the day before, Margaret escorted Cass into another one where the dogs were housed in pens with fenced runs. Cass shoved her shaking hands down into her coat pockets. She didn't want anyone to see that her hands were trembling.

Margaret stopped in front of the first cage. "The dogs on this side of the building are the ones we call the 'reimagined' dogs. They're working dogs that we get from all over the world. When they're too old we take in the ones we can, retrain them and give them new purpose. Esme also has a breeding program for specialized therapy dogs for epilepsy and dia-betes patients. We train from puppy age until they are just over a year old. Those dogs are

Labrador retrievers, Labradoodles and golden retrievers."

Cass nodded.

"Now, this is Oscar. He's a sweet dog and has been paired with Mr. Ellis."

"I've seen them together some." Cass recognized the small black and white, wire-haired dog, along with a number of others. They'd all been paired with patients at the clinic.

"And you should remember this one. He's the dog I understand that you and Lyle brought in the other night. We're calling him Dougal."

Cass nodded. Dougal suited the little dog. Rufus had already been named when Cass had got him, but his name had suited him too.

They moved to the next pen. The dogs were getting larger as they went.

"This is Morrow. He used to be a guide dog."

He was being "reimagined," much as Cass was working to do with her life. If she didn't return to search and rescue, what was she going to do? Could she accept a new partner and try again? A sick feeling welled up in her, but she forced it down with a clenched jaw. She'd already made a spectacle of herself in front of Lyle. She *would not* do the same in Margaret's presence.

Margaret kept moving down the aisle, intro-

ducing Cass to dogs as they went. Cass battled
to remain calm rather than listening until Margaret said, "...and he was a search and rescue
dog. A good one, I understand. But he went
blind in one eye and that ended his career."

Cass's attention remained riveted to the
light-gray-furred German shepherd lying quietly in the back corner of the cage.

"He hasn't adjusted to being here as we
would like. I think we're rather dull to him
after his exciting life." Margaret's voice was
sympathetic.

Cass empathized with the dog's pain. She,
too, was out of her comfort zone for reasons
beyond her control.

"Now, this is McDuff. Everyone's favorite."
A big dog with shaggy fur and wide brown
eyes came to greet them.

Cass reached out to him without thinking.
He smelled her hand, fluffy tail wagging.

"Now that you've met everyone I'll show
you where the supplies are and tell you some of
your duties. I have to admit you're the first resident to offer to help us with dog care and I'm
very glad to have you. We don't have enough
help."

Margaret showed Cass the room where
food was stored, the grooming area and where
cleaning tools could be found. She explained

what Cass needed to do and on which days of the week. "Also, we would like you to walk any dogs that don't currently have assignments. That's the list on the board over here." She walked to the wall where a clipboard hung. "Currently there are just three dogs. You're free to take them outside for a walk on the lead or a run in the outdoor pen."

Cass would turn them out in the pen. Leash walking was more than she was emotionally prepared for. Too personal, too risky. She might start caring.

"You think you'll be okay with the work?" Margaret checked her watch.

Cass nodded. This she could do. She would be active instead of sitting around with a dog in her lap or on the floor beside her. Surely she wouldn't get attached tending to all the dogs on a daily basis. Having one assigned to her was the danger. She could feed them, walk them, and clean their cages and meet her therapy requirements then move on. All she had to do was make up her mind to do what she had to do. For some people that type of work might be beneath them. But it was the perfect means for Cass to ease back into interacting with a dog without the temptation of completely committing.

Over the next hour she fed and watered the

dogs. When it was time to enter the search and rescue dog's cage, she had to read his name on the sign because she'd missed it when Margaret had said it earlier. She hesitated. Hero didn't scare her, instead he reminded her too much of herself. He remained in that corner as if he wanted to shut the world out. Was that what she was doing?

"Hey, fellow, it's nice to meet you. I understand we've been in the same business. I'm sorry to hear about your eye. That's tough." She moved to fill his food bowl. He watched her closely as she worked. Cass filled his water bowl from a bucket. He came up on his haunches as if he might be thirsty. "Come and get it. I won't hurt you."

"He mostly speaks German."

Cass heart clinched. Just like Rufus.

"I should have told you that." Margaret stood outside the cage. "But I'm sure he appreciates your soothing voice. I've been watching. You're good with the dogs."

"I've been around them all my life." Cass unlocked the cage.

"It shows. It's time for you to go." Margaret held the gate to the cage open. "I don't want to wear you out on your first day. I'll see you tomorrow."

"Okay. I need to put some things away before I go." Cass walked back toward the storeroom.

"Can you see yourself out?" Margaret called, heading the other way.

Cass placed the bucket she carried on the floor. "I can."

"Good. You did well today, Cass." Margaret gave her a smile and left.

Hopefully each day would get easier.

Three days later Cass was on the minibus to the village with five other residents. She looked out the window at the beautiful and fascinating countryside. She'd seen much of the world and, even covered in patches of snow, this place appealed to her. Her doctors had been wise to send her here.

Going to the canine therapy center still didn't fill her with excitement but it wasn't as difficult as it had been on the first day. She'd managed to interact with the dogs while remaining emotionally removed from them. She was pleased to see that Dougal was growing stronger each day. His odd appearance with some weight on him was beginning to make him look cute. The only dog that did disturb her was Hero. He still remained standoffish. Cass was trying not to let it bother her, yet it did.

Today she wasn't going to think about dogs

or therapy or even the past. Instead she was going to enjoy her trip to the village. She didn't know what to expect of Cluchlochry, but she was enchanted from the moment she stepped off the bus. It looked like a scene from a Victorian Christmas card. Wreaths of fresh greenery with bows were on every building door and window. The main road was just large enough for two small narrow vehicles to pass. Her large American SUV would never be able to make it.

The sun was shining this morning, promising a warmer day than usual, and she was glad she'd left Lyle's scarf and hat behind, not wanting to have to carry them.

In the center of the village just feet from where she'd stepped off the bus was the cobblestoned village square. She followed the crowd to a building she'd overheard was called the community center. There were a number of tents set up outside, but Cass found the majority of the stalls inside. The individual areas each had their own holiday decorations. It was like entering a winter wonderland. Excitement filled her at the thought of some retail therapy. She wasn't much of a "girly-girl" where most things were concerned, but she did love a shopping trip. The van had come in early enough that the crowd was still comfortably small. Visiting the stalls should be fun.

She planned to buy boots and socks today as Lyle had suggested that first night. However, she would wait until later to shop for them to avoid carrying them around any longer than necessary. After she was finished at the Christmas market she would ask someone where to do shoe shopping. For now, she was going to see what the market had to offer.

The first stall she came to held handmade wooden figurines. Behind the table sat an older, grizzled man with the air of an outdoorsman. He glanced up for a moment then went back to whittling.

Cass picked up an angel and admired the workmanship. The texture was smooth and there was attention to detail. The face had the kind of expression befitting an angel. It was old-world craftsmanship at its best. Her mother would love any of the items on display. She would return to buy something for her mother before she headed back to the castle. Hoping she would make it home before Christmas, she planned on being prepared to celebrate with her family.

When they'd heard she was injured they had wanted to come to her in Germany. She had convinced them not to, assuring them she was going to be fine. Once she'd been sent to therapy she had persuaded them she would be home sooner if she concentrated on getting better. What she hadn't said was that she needed time to recover emotionally so she wouldn't fall apart in front of them, as she had with Lyle.

Cass paused at every stall, fearing that if she didn't she might miss something. At this rate she wouldn't see all the market today and would still climb back on the bus with an armload of purchases. However, she needed to get some local money to buy things. She went outside to the street and searched for an ATM sign. Soon she had some pounds in her pocket. Conscious of smiling for the first time in a long while she went to the nearest stall.

This one offered handmade Christmas-tree ornaments. Cass was enthralled. Each one unique, they were made out of natural things like nuts, twigs, and pine cones. They would be perfect on a tree. Once again she resisted the impulse to buy and moved on to the next display.

There she found leather goods of quality craftsmanship. She continued walking, merely looking at some stalls and handling items at others. Coming to town had been a good decision, even though she had initially intended only to buy new walking boots and socks.

Nevertheless she was having a nice day. Even the bustle of the growing crowd made her feel more alive. She had needed this kind of therapy.

Spying a sign with the words "Aileen's Knitting" on it, she made her way over. It was past time to return Lyle's hat and scarf but Cass wanted to get her own before she did so. And some gloves.

The stall had two tables and a number of hat racks filled with hats and scarfs of every color. Cass went to one of the tables and ran her hand over a few of the items of outerwear, even trying on a couple. She studied herself in a mirror hung on a stand to see how she looked. The pale pink and gray striped scarf and matching solid pink hat she especially liked.

A plump middle-aged woman sat behind the table next to a small heater. Her needles clicked as she spoke. "That looks lovely on you."

Her Scottish brogue was so thick Cass had to concentrate to understand her. "Thank you. Your work is beautiful. And so soft." Cass pulled the cap off and picked up another in the same color but with a rosette on the side. She studied it.

At that moment a familiar masculine shoulder pushed a door open just behind the woman. Lyle entered, carrying a box. He turned and the door closed. She must have caught his eye because he looked at her with surprise. A smile curved his lips that made her middle flutter. "Well, hi, there. I see you took my suggestion about coming to the market."

Her face warmed. This was their first encounter since they had kissed. Surely if she acted like it hadn't happened, he would as well. "Yeah, I'm doing some shopping therapy, like the doctor ordered."

Lyle looked over the box at her. "I wouldn't say I ordered it, but I'm glad you came."

She nodded toward the box. "I see you're moonlighting. You don't have enough jobs already?"

He chuckled as he rested the corner of the box on the edge of the table, continuing to hold it. "It's more like helping my mother out. Muscles and all that."

Cass knew those muscles well. She had felt those strong arms around her and the firmness of his chest when she'd pressed her face against it. She glanced at Lyle's mother, who watched them with pronounced interest, her knitting momentarily forgotten.

Lyle's head turned as if following Cass's line of sight. "Mum, this is Cass Bellow. She's one of our residents at the castle. Cass, my mother, Aileen Sinclair."

Cass was unsure how to respond. Lyle's mother was looking between the two of them as if she suspected something Cass was refusing to admit to herself. A second too late to sound natural, Cass finally managed to get out, "It's nice to meet you. Your work really is lovely. I wish I had your talent."

The door opened again and a tall man who was undoubtedly an older version of Lyle joined them with a box in his hands. "Aileen, where do you want this?

"Over in the corner will be fine." Lyle's mother pointed to the one opposite hers. "I don't want it near the heater."

The man put the box down as instructed and turned to Cass. Something about his bearing made Cass want to stand at attention and pass inspection yet he looked in poor health. His was gaunt, far too thin for his height. There wasn't a sparkle in his eyes like Lyle's. His skin had a grayish tint to it. Lyle's father was sick.

"Sir, this is Cass Bellow. My father, retired Colonel Gregor Sinclair."

Still resisting the urge to salute, she settled for, "Hello, sir."

"Hello, young lady." The older man offered his hand. Cass put hers inside his. He still had a firm grip, but his fingers felt fragile in hers.

She looked at Lyle's parents. "It's nice to meet you both."

"You're not from around here, I can tell," Lyle's father said.

Cass chortled. "Is it that obvious? No, I'm from America. Montana currently."

Lyle's father nodded. "I worked with many Americans while I was in the military. Good sorts. I expect that Lyle will be working with some as well when he returns to active duty."

Her look swung to Lyle. Was he going to join the army again? He seemed to love working at the clinic.

Before she could ask, he took the hat from her hand. "This will look nice on you."

She unwrapped the scarf from her neck. "I think so too. I'd like to get both of them, and the gloves as well. They're too nice to pass up. Plus I need to return yours."

"You do?" Lyle's mother gave him a questioning look.

"Cass didn't have a chance to prepare for our Scottish weather before she was transferred here." Lyle turned to put his box on top of the other one as if discouraging more of his mother's questions.

Cass pulled out her cash, counted out the correct amount indicated on a sign next to the mirror, then handed it across the table.

"Thank you, Mrs. Sinclair. Maybe one day I'll learn to knit and make something half as lovely as your work."

"If you'd like to learn I could show you. Lyle could bring you to the house some day for lunch." Lyle's mother looked from Cass to her son, a small smile on her lips.

Was Aileen's maternal intuition working overtime? Cass shook her head. "Oh, no, I didn't mean to imply you should teach me."

"Nonsense. I'd love to give you a lesson. And at this time of the year knitting is about all I'm doing anyway, with the Christmas market going until the season is over." The clicking of the needles started again.

Cass didn't know what to think about Aileen's invitation but she said the polite thing. "Thank you."

"Would you like a bag for those?" Mrs. Sinclair asked, a nod of her head indicating the knitted items Cass held.

Cass glanced down. "No, I think I'll wear them." She stuffed the gloves in her pocket, looped the scarf around her neck again and pulled the hat snugly over her head. "It was nice to meet you Colonel and Mrs. Sinclair." Giving Lyle a swift look as she turned to leave, she added, "Bye." Hesitating a second, she turned to look at Lyle. "Would you mind giving me directions to where I can buy some boots?"

"Why don't I show you instead?" he offered.

"I don't want to put you out. I'm sure your mother needs your help." Cass didn't need him thinking she was using that as a ploy to spend more time with him.

"I'm good for now." Aileen waved a hand. "While you're gone, Lyle, why don't you stop by McKinney's Pub and get Cass one of their pies?" She looked directly at Cass. "Best meat pies you'll find anywhere."

Lyle stepped around the table and came to stand beside Cass. His hand touched her back briefly and was gone. He called over his shoulder to his mother, "I'll do it."

They worked their way around the people coming and going as they walked in the direction of the door. A couple of times Lyle put a gentle hand in the small of her back while guiding her through the crowd.

"That hat and scarf color is very flattering on you," he said. "Reminds me of when you blush. Your cheeks turn that shade." He grinned as their gazes met. "Like right now."

The compliment gave her a luscious warm throughout her body like a hot drink heating her from the inside out.

They exited the building and turned left

down the street. As they continued walking toward the other end of the village green they approached a monument. It consisted of a tall narrow shaft encircled by steps. On top was a small statue.

"What's this?" Cass stopped and studied it.

"It's a Mercat Cross. They have been used in Scotland since the eleven-hundreds to distinguish the right by the monarch to hold a market or fair. They were symbols of authority. There're aren't many of them left now. We're rather proud of ours."

"That's interesting." She liked learning historical facts about places she went.

"They're not only places for merchants to meet but places where state and civic proclamations would be made. Even to this day in Edinburgh the town crier will still make proclamations on occasions."

She looked up to where the statue stood on top. "I would love to hear one sometime."

"Maybe you will one day."

Cass doubted that. She wouldn't be here long enough for that to happen.

They moved on in comfortable silence until they made their way through the crowd and out into the open again.

"So how have your last few days of working with the dogs gone?"

Cass glanced over at him. "Don't you already know? I figured you've been checking up on me."

Lyle chuckled. "I have, but I'd like to hear from you."

She appreciated his honestly. "It's going better than I expected. I admit it was tough to get started, but I'm getting used to the dogs and them to me."

"I'm glad to hear that." He did sound pleased, as if her happiness really mattered to him.

She couldn't say she was happy yet, but she'd moved the needle that direction. "You're not really surprised, are you?"

"Not really. Canine therapy has proved very effective. Even on those who are resistant." He gave her a knowing look.

"Is that your way of saying I told you so?" Somehow she didn't mind if he did. This was the best she had felt since before the accident. Her thoughts weren't so dark anymore.

Lyle stopped in front of a shop built of brown timber. The upper half of the door had four window panes. A Christmas wreath hung low beneath the glass. Attached above the door was a swag of greenery entwined with red ribbon. On either side of the door were display windows filled with boots, coats and other outdoor wear. All of it was arranged to create the impression of presents under a Christmas tree.

Lyle opened the door for her. "The shoes are at the back on the right."

Cass followed him down a narrow aisle lined with high shelves stuffed with items. The dim lighting added to the alluring atmosphere. The place smelled of wood oil and pine. Cass inhaled, taking it deep into her lungs. It reminded her of Lyle. She was enchanted with the shop. In fact, she was charmed by everything about the Heatherglen area, including Lyle. What was happening to her?

They arrived at the back of the shop. There in one corner was a small wooden bench along with boxes of boots piled on the floor.

Lyle stretched to his full height and looked over the shelves. "Apparently Mr. Stewart isn't around. We'll have a look at these and he should be back soon. He must have stepped out for lunch. I have experience with this so we'll just help ourselves."

Cass lowered her chin, eyeing him dubiously. "You've been a shoe salesman?"

He gave her an indignant look. "I worked here when I came home on school breaks."

"Oh. So you *are* a jack-of-all-trades."

He stepped toward the boxes. "I wouldn't

exactly say that, but I can handle reading shoe-
boxes. What's your size?"

"Eight and a half, US." She sat on the bench.

Lyle nodded and studied them a moment.
Moving a couple, he pulled one out. "I hope
I made the European to American conversion
correctly. Give these a try and we'll see."

She took the box from him and opened it.
Removing her shoes, Cass pulled the new boot
on her right foot. She stood and wiggled her
toes. "Nicely done. Feels good but I would really rather have them in black."

"I aim to please. Let me see what I can find."
Lyle shifted around a few boxes. With a bright
smile on his handsome face, he handed her a
box.

Cass sat on the bench again and started trying on the second boot.

"What's your favorite color?" Lyle asked,
his back to her as he straightened boxes.

"Why?"

"You need some good socks." He studied
her with visible curiosity.

She continued trying on her new boots.
"Blue."

He moved down the wall and seconds later
handed her a pair of thick socks. "These'll
keep your feet warm and wick the moisture
away. I promise you'll like them."

Cass removed the boots and her socks then pulled on the new ones. "I can already tell the difference." She flexed her foot then slipped her foot into the boot. Nice. Quickly she pulled on the other boot and laced them both up.

Standing, she walked back and forth a couple of times, testing the feel of the footwear. "You know, if you ever decide to give up medicine you could have a future as a personal shopper."

Lyle gave a regal bow. "Thank you. I have to say with complete confidence that's the first time anyone has suggested that to me."

They both laughed.

When was the last time she'd laughed like this? How had she not noticed it slipping away?

She liked Lyle's relaxed view of life. With his job and military background she marveled he wasn't uptight and domineering. Instead he seemed to accept life as it came and made the most of it whenever he could. Cass needed more of that in her world.

Lyle had a way of making her smile, and she also needed more of that right now. However, she must not start depending on him to make her feel better. She had to depend on herself. She had to regain her strength. Be strong.

If she opened up to him any further, leaving him would be a new trauma, one she knew she couldn't handle. Her job certainly didn't lend itself to an easygoing and emotional personality. Even when she was at home her focus had been on working with Rufus to keep them both sharp. Had the men in her life been right? Did she live too closed off? Had been concentrating on her job and Rufus more than she should have?

"You want to keep those on?" He picked up the box.

"I believe I will. Start breaking them in." Cass picked up her other shoes and placed them in the box while Lyle held it. She met his gaze. "By the way, what's your favorite color?"

"Green." His eyes didn't waver. "I'm particularly fond of the shade of green of your eyes."

Her breath caught. "Are you flirting with me?"

"What if I am?" He took the box and set it on the bench. "I've been thinking about that kiss."

A tingle ran through her. "You shouldn't."

"What? Think about it or think about doing it again?"

"Both, " she squeaked.

"Why?" His voice turned gravelly, went soft. Lyle stepped toward her.

Because she was damaged. Because she was scared. Because she couldn't handle caring about anything or anyone again. "Because I'm leaving soon."

"Cass, we can share an interest in each other without it becoming a lifelong commitment. I'd like to get to know you better. Couldn't we be friends? Enjoy each other's company while you're here?"

Put that way, it sounded reasonable. Lyle moved so close that his heat warmed her. Why was it so hard to breathe? She simmered with anticipation. His hands came to rest at her waist as his mouth lowered to hers.

She didn't want his kiss. That wasn't true. Until that moment she'd had no idea how desperately she did want Lyle's lips on hers. Her breath caught as his mouth made a light brush over hers. He pulled away. Cass ran her tongue over her bottom lip, tasting him.

Lyle groaned and pulled her tight against his chest. His lips firmly settled over hers. Cass grabbed his shoulders to steady herself. Slowly she went up on her toes, her desire drawing her nearer to him. Sweet heat curled and twisted through her center and seeped into her every cell. She'd found her cozy fire in a winter storm.

The sound of the door opening brought both their heads up. Their gazes locked with each other's.

"Hello? Is someone here?" a man called.

"It's Lyle, Mr. Stewart. I'm in the boot section."

"Please don't do that again," Cass whispered, and stepped as far away as the small space would allow. She couldn't deal with the feelings swarming in her. This wasn't what she needed or wanted. She needed to figure out her life, not complicate it.

Now that she'd really been kissed by Lyle, she wanted more. *No!* And she couldn't handle the feelings his kiss had kindled in her. This was too much at the wrong time. Panic welled in her. She shook her head. Letting something grow between them would only turn into disaster. She didn't want to hurt Lyle, and she couldn't endure another heartache.

He studied her for a moment, then picked up the box, placing it under his arm as if nothing earthshaking had happened. "Let's go and pay for these then get one of those pies."

That suited her just fine. She could pretend nothing had changed as well as he did. Head held high, she followed him two aisles over to a wooden counter. A middle-aged man with white tuffs of hair, rosy cheeks and a white beard stood behind it. He could pass for a Santa Claus.

"Well, hello. How're you, Lyle?" Mr. Stewart gave them both a wide smile.

The man's accent was just as thick as Lyle's mother's.

"Fine, thanks, Mr. Stewart. We've been helping ourselves to some boots. I was just going to write you a note and leave the money."

"Give me a second to set this down." The older man placed a brown bag on the counter. "I went to get a meat pie before they were all gone. I look forward to Mrs. McKinney's pies all year."

"I hope you left some for Cass and me. We're on our way there next." Lyle leaned toward the bag and inhaled deeply. "Mrs. McKinney makes the best."

While the men were talking, Cass managed to get her purchase paid for. She and Lyle exited the shop. The sun was shining but clouds were gathering.

"It looks like it'll snow again tonight," Lyle commented. "We need to go this way." He indicated to the left. "McKinney's Pub is down this way."

Cass shook her head. "I'm not really hungry. I think I'll just look around some more then go back to the castle. I appreciate your help with my boots."

Lyle said nothing until she looked at him.

"Cass, I didn't mean to make things uncomfortable between us."

"You didn't."

He searched her face for a long moment. "Then you won't mind joining me for lunch. You don't want me to have to eat alone."

She pursed her lips. "Somewhere in there I think there's a touch of emotional blackmail."

He quirked a brow, his grin devious. "Could be. Live dangerously and join me."

She was doing that by just being around him. Her body still hummed with awareness, but she did owe him. He'd been nothing but kind. More than once Lyle had gone far beyond what was necessary. Helping her with her new boots was just one of the small things. Still feeling unsteady after their kiss, she was afraid that remaining in Lyle's presence might further break her tightly strung nerves. It was risky to her well-being for her to say yes. "If you're going to insist."

A winning smile lit up his face. "I am. You know how I hate to eat alone. This way."

They didn't walk far before they came to a building with an elaborate sign stating that it was McKinney's Pub above the door. "Here we are."

Cass turned the doorknob and pushed the door open, to find a room with a dark timber-beamed ceiling, stone-flagged floor and a handful of wooden tables and chairs unoccupied. Men were standing at the bar with drinks and talking. She glanced back at Lyle to see him duck to enter.

"Why don't you go see if you can find us a table near the fire while I place our order?"

"Okay."

"Before you go, would you prefer beef or pork?" Lyle asked.

"I don't know. You make the call." She didn't often let others decide anything for her. Being with Lyle was definitely having an odd effect on her. For some reason she trusted him not to let her down.

"Okay. One more thing, hot drink or something cold?"

"Hot, definitely hot." She shivered. "I can't even imagine drinking something cold." Cass reached into her pocket. "Here's money for mine."

Lyle looked offended. "Put that away. I'll get this."

"I don't expect you to buy my lunch." She couldn't continue being indebted to him. "You're always doing something for me."

"You can return the favor sometime. Now, go and find us a seat." He started toward the bar.

"You don't need my help carrying the food?"

He shook his head. "I can handle it. You find us a place to sit before they're all taken."

"All right." Cass made her way to an empty table to one side of the roaring fire in the fireplace. She turned a chair toward the flames and sat down, stretching out her hands to the warmth. A couple of minutes later she looked around to see where Lyle was.

She quickly found him among the people at the bar. With his height and broad shoulders he stood out among the others. His hair was mussed but it matched his easygoing personality. Lyle was every bit as appealing to look at as he was to talk to. She was getting in deeper and deeper the longer she was with him. As hard as she tried to push away, the greater the pull he had on her.

Soon, carrying two drinks with steam wafting from them, Lyle joined her. He placed them on the table. "You got us a perfect table. How did you manage that?"

Cass shrugged and picked up her mug. "Lucky, I guess."

Lyle picked his mug up as well. "This is hot punch. I think you'll like it."

She took a sip. "Mmm…"

"I like it when you make that sound," he said, just for her ears. "You did it a while ago when I kissed you."

"I did not!"

Lyle gave her a wicked smile that said, *Do you want to bet?*

Heat that had nothing to do with the punch surged through her. "You shouldn't say things like that to me."

"What, the truth?"

Much to her relief, they were interrupted by a young woman placing two plates on the table.

Lyle said politely, "Thank you." The woman gave him a shy look and hurried away.

It appeared Lyle sent most women into a tailspin by just being nice. Cass had imagined he only had that effect on her.

She watched as Lyle used a napkin to pick up the perfect brown half-moon pastry. He closed his eyes and took a bite. His eyelids dropped as an expression of pure bliss washed over his face. He slowly chewed. Something low within Cass tightened. She shook off the vision of Lyle naked in bed, wearing that same expression. How could just two kisses cause such an idea to pop into her head?

Instead of concentrating on her traitor of a mind, she followed Lyle's lead and picked up her pie. She took a small bite of the flaky pastry. It melted on her tongue as the taste of tangy beef hit her taste buds. She closed her eyes and enjoyed the moment. Did she have the same look on her face as Lyle? She opened hers to find him watching her closely, an intense flame of desire in his eyes. Oh, yeah, she had.

His voice turned husky as he said, "You should look like that all the time."

"How's that?" Cass dared to ask, unable to take her gaze off him.

"Angelic, as if you had found nirvana."

Emotion that had nothing to do eating meat pie and everything to do with the fire in Lyle's eyes flashed through her. This caring and comforting man wanted her. That knowledge was empowering.

"Hello, Lyle." a woman's soft voice said from behind Cass.

The pleasure lighting Lyle's face went out, leaving a blank look with a hint of surprise. The woman was important to Lyle. Cass turned to see her. She had vivid blue eyes and was heavily pregnant. A sick feeling filled her stomach. Who was the woman to Lyle?

The last person Lyle had expected to see was Freya. He hadn't seen her for some time. Through his mother and father, he'd learned that she had married and moved to Fort William. He was truly glad for her, but that didn't make the surprise of seeing her again any less nerve rattling.

He laid his food down and stood. "Freya."

"It's nice to see you, Lyle." She sounded hesitant, as if she was afraid of his reaction. "How are you?"

"Well. And you?"

Her hand went to rest on her protruding middle. "I'm doing fine."

Lyle felt a sharp, piercing pain. They had talked about and planned on now many children they would have. There had been so many dreams they'd shared. He mentally shook his head. Those were long gone. Their relationship had been doomed the minute he'd boarded the train for training camp. He knew that now, but back then he'd been too caught up in pleasing his father by joining the army and the image of his fiancée waiting on his glorious return to see reality. Knowing his own mind and what he wanted out of life hadn't entered the equation. Much less fighting for it.

Freya glanced at Cass, who was observing them with interest. Was Cass thinking the child was his? "Freya." He nodded toward Cass. "This is Cass Bellow. Freya is an old friend."

"Hello," Freya said with a small smile as the two women studied each other.

A man not much taller than Freya but with huge shoulders joined them. He studied Lyle then Cass before giving Freya a questioning look, his brows making a V at his nose.

Freya cleared her throat. "This is Angus, my husband."

Lyle extend his hand. "Lyle Sinclair." It took a second before the man's eyes widened in recognition, then narrowed.

Angus shook Lyle's hand briefly, then put his arm across Freya's shoulders in a statement of ownership. To her he said, "Your parents are waiting."

Freya gave Lyle a sad, apologetic look. "It was nice to see you, Lyle."

"You too, Freya." He watched them walk away. That had certainly been interesting. Why had the meeting left him feeling so disconcerted? He'd got over Freya years ago, yet it still shook him to see her again. At one time they had been so close. Now there was a fence between them so high that they would never be able to climb it. Her husband's actions and facial expression made him question how controlling and overly jealous he might be. Was Freya truly happy?

"I think it's time for me to get back to the castle." Cass stood. "I promised Flora I would help with some of the decorations today instead of formal therapy."

Lyle blinked. How had he forgotten Cass

was there? She must think him an idiot. "But we haven't finished our meal."

She gave him a curious look. "I have. Thank you for the pie. I should go."

"I'll walk you to the minibus." He needed to answer the questions hanging between them.

Cass waved for him to sit down. "No, you finish your lunch. I can find my way. I'll see you back at the castle."

Before he could order his thoughts, she was gone.

What was Cass thinking? Imagining? Had she seen what had once been between him and Freya?

CHAPTER SIX

BACK AT THE castle Cass debated whether or not to return Lyle's coat and other belongings that evening or wait until she saw him during work hours. Surely he needed his clothes. Yet her growing curiosity about the history between him and Freya made her cautious about seeking him out. It really wasn't her business, and yet she couldn't dismiss the distinct impression that something between them had caused Lyle great pain. Or was the baby the issue?

She knew Lyle well enough to know he would take responsibility for a child he'd fathered. Having a family of his own would be a serious matter to him. So was the baby his?

As hard as Cass had tried to maintain her emotional distance from Lyle, she cared about him. He had made it impossible for her to remain uninterested. Not only did she find him attractive, he had also proved he was a good man. So here she was, caring about him, concerned for him.

The feeling he needed someone to talk to also nagged at her. She owed him. Maybe she could help.

With her new socks and boots on and wearing her own jacket, which she'd found a few days ago laid out on her bed, she bundled Lyle's coat, socks, scarf and hat in her arms and made her way out of the castle. It would soon be dark, so she had tucked her flashlight safely in her pocket for the return trip.

At the gate leading into his yard she stopped. Was she being too forward by coming to his home like this? What would he think about her just showing up? Still, the need to see him, be there for him if he needed to talk, neutralized her apprehension. Her outlook on life had improved so much since he'd let her spill her problems to him. Maybe tonight he needed someone to listen to his troubles. She owed him and cared about him enough that she should at least be here for him. They were friends.

Pausing in the act of knocking on the door, she had the uneasy feeling her "honorable" thoughts about Lyle needing her were just an excuse to see him again. He had friends, colleagues, even his parents to confide in, so what had possessed her to think he required her?

As if of its own accord her fist hit the door. Breath held, she listened for movement inside, half wishing Lyle wasn't home, half hoping he was. All of this was so against her nature. She'd always known her own mind. Why was she doubting herself now? Why had she started acting like a silly schoolgirl around Lyle?

She had stepped off the porch to leave when the door opened. Her heart beat faster as she straightened her back.

"Cass?" He sounded both startled and pleased.

Did he think she was seeking his interest by showing up like this? Was she? "I, uh, wanted to return your things now I have my jacket back and a new scarf and hat." She thrust them into his hands before turning away.

"Would you like to come in for some coffee?" He asked, sounding hopeful.

She looked at him, even less sure about being there. But hadn't she been eager for Lyle to invite her in? "Could we make that tea?"

He chuckled. "Of course. Come in."

Inside, Lyle helped her off with her coat. As he did so, his hands rested on her shoulders for a moment. She missed the heaviness of them the second they were gone. She had the impression he wanted to keep an appropriate distance between them. Wasn't that what she'd all but told him she wanted? Especially after their kiss in the shop. Or did she want that?

"Come and join me in the kitchen," Lyle suggested as he moved through the door opposite the living room.

"Let me take my boots off first. They're pretty muddy." Cass sat on the small bench underneath the coat rack and removed them, then followed him.

Lyle was already at the stove with the kettle in his hand when she entered. He placed it on the element and leaned against the counter. "I see you're wearing your new socks again."

"Yes. They're the best I've ever worn. I plan to buy a few more pairs before I leave for home." Cass settled into one of the wooden chairs at the small round table in the middle of the room.

"Flora tells me that if you continue making the progress you have been, it'll be sooner rather than later." He opened a tin filled with biscuits and placed it on the table before returning to the cabinets.

She reached for a biscuit. "I'm pretty determined to get through this as quickly as possible."

Lyle glanced over his shoulder, studying her for a moment. What was he thinking? He returned to removing mugs from an upper cabinet and added tea bags to them. "I noticed that."

Did it bother him that she so was eager to leave the clinic? Cass looked around. "I like your kitchen."

"Thanks." He put a bowl of sugar and small pitcher of milk on the table. The kettle switched itself off as the water was boiling. Lyle poured the steaming water into the mugs before setting one in front of her and the other at the place beside her, rather than across from her. He took a seat.

She liked him being close enough to touch. Maybe she had imagined he was trying to keep distance between them.

Lyle pushed the tin in her direction. "Have another if you wish. It's interesting you like my kitchen. These old cottage kitchens have charm but they're often difficult to modernize. I've been led to believe women like to have the latest and greatest to work with."

Cass added sugar and milk to her tea. "That sounds like you're speaking from personal experience."

"Yeah. Freya always wanted one of those new brick houses with all the glass."

A zip ran along Cass's nerves. He had made it that easy for her to ask about Freya. Still, she hesitated to pry. Would he be upset if she did? Cass watched him. Lyle studied his tea. "Would that be the Freya I met today?"

"That's the one." A pensive look remained on his face. "I think I owe you an explanation."

"Why?"

"Because I was kissing you and then a pregnant woman who I'm sure you figured out shared a past with me shows up. It didn't make me look good."

"You didn't—don't—owe me an explanation." No matter how much she wanted to hear one.

"Maybe not, but I'd like to give you one anyway. The baby isn't mine. I haven't seen Freya in over a year. She was my girlfriend when we were teenagers. I asked her to be my wife the night before I left for basic training."

"Now I understand the look on her husband's face." It had been jealousy.

Lyle nodded. "Yeah, I'm not his favorite person, I imagine. But he has nothing to worry about. It's been over for a long time."

"What happened?" Cass hissed in dismay. "I shouldn't have asked that. It's not my business."

He finally met her look. "It doesn't matter. I don't want to have any secrets from you."

What was he saying? That sounded too

much like he wanted a relationship more intimate than friendship. Their kisses had certainly been a step beyond mere friends.

"I received the classic 'Dear John' letter. By the time I was able to come home months later she was already married."

Cass placed her hand over his hand resting on the table. She had been right. He did need to talk. "I'm sorry that happened to you. You deserved better."

He turned over his hand and held hers. "It was a rotten feeling at the time but far better than marrying the wrong person."

She couldn't disagree with him, but it must have been a horribly painful experience. To feel so helpless. She knew that all feeling too well. In too many areas of her life.

"It took me some time, but I realized that we would never have made it. Ours was a young immature love and an engagement based on me leaving, not on something lasting. I promised myself that the next time I asked a woman to marry me, we would both be mature enough to know what we were doing, and that we understood what real love is." He let go of her hand.

"Enough of this serious talk. Here I am dragging up my long-gone past while your tea is getting cold."

Cass took a sip from her mug. "I knew something big had gone on between the two of you. I just wasn't sure what. Her husband made a point of making it clear where she belonged."

"I noticed that as well. I hope she's happy. My mother said this is her second child." He bit into a cookie.

"I must admit I was curious. In fact, half of the reason I came tonight was that I thought you might need to talk. You helped me by listening so I thought I could return the favor."

He gave her a thoughtful look then grinned. "I see. And here I was thinking you wanted to spend more time with me."

Just like that Lyle had changed the atmosphere. He knew how to ease a tense situation.

She returned his smile. "Please don't let anyone tell you that you lack an ego."

His grin turned suggestive, causing her middle to quiver. "I'm not sure that was a compliment, but I'm going to choose to take it that way."

Cass huffed in humor. "Does anything keep you down long?"

"I try to keep a positive outlook where I can. I learned long ago that life was easier that way. How do you see the glass? Half full or half empty?"

She winced in her mind. Most of her life

she would have said half full but right now she wasn't sure she could. "Can I get back to you on that?"

Lyle watched her far too closely for comfort. "Sure. I just want you to know that I'm here for you."

"Thanks. I know I showed up at the castle with a chip on my shoulder. I'm trying to do better."

"From all I've heard, you are."

Cass pushed away from the table. "I should be going."

"Do you have to? Stay awhile and I'll walk you back later." His face was hopeful.

She ought to leave. Hadn't she already stepped over the line by coming here? Yet she did want to remain longer. "I guess I could."

"Great. Would you like to watch TV, play chess or maybe do a puzzle?"

She blinked and laughed. "Wow, you know how to show a woman a wild time."

He carried their mugs to the sink. "What can I say? Most of my excitement comes from accidents. I'm not planning one to impress you."

"I'll be more than happy to settle for a puzzle. I haven't done one of those in a long time." That seemed like a safe enough activity.

"During the winter months I keep one going all the time. It's in the living room. Go on in and see what you can do. I'll be in after I finish here." He turned to the sink.

Cass did as he suggested. A fire was burning. She found the table with the puzzle laid out on it behind the sofa. It had to have been there the other night but she had been so out of it she hadn't noticed. The puzzle was a picture of a lioness and her cub. A difficult one at best. She sat in the chair, adjusting the lamp over the table to shine it where she wanted it.

Lyle entered to find Cass sitting in his chair at his puzzle table. Something about the sight seemed right. She looked like she belonged, fit in his world.

Her head remained lowered. The glow of the fire reflected off her hair. He longed to brush his hand across it. Test its softness. Pulling another chair close, he joined her.

"So this is how you spend your evenings?" She picked a piece up and tried it. It didn't fit. She put it down and went for another.

"Not every evening." He wished Cass would put as much energy into getting to know him as she was into working on the puzzle. Was he really that desperate for a woman? No, it was more about the sensations Cass stirred in him. Sensations that had lain dormant for a long time. The same ones he'd been afraid to show for so long.

"I would think a hot young doctor would be too busy with the ladies at the pub to spend time doing puzzles." She put a piece in and made a tiny sound of joy, and it sparked something in him.

What would it be like to kiss her again? That thought was all it took to set his blood humming. How would she react if he tried to kiss her right now? Would she push him away or tug him closer, like she had at the shop? He had to stop these runaway thoughts.

Focus on the puzzle, he told himself. Concentrate on finding that one missing piece. Maybe if he did that, he'd forget the sweet smell of Cass's hair moving just inches from him, or the breathiness of her voice when she spoke or the soft touch of her hand as it brushed his when they both tried to fit a piece into the same space.

Minutes ticked by, the longing in him growing, groaning with the seconds. To stop himself from reaching for Cass, Lyle stood and went to the fireplace, using the need to put another log on the fire as an excuse. With his back to the warmth, he watched her. She truly was striking. Every fiber of his being was on alert for the least hint of encouragement.

Cass looked up. "Hey, are you going to leave all of this to me? This is such a great picture."

"I like the one I'm seeing." His gaze met hers and held.

Cass's head dipped to the side as if she was making a decision. Moments ticked by as they watched each other.

Lyle cleared his throat. "Cass, I've been thinking of little else but kissing you again. If you don't want that to happen then it might be better if you go."

She blinked. "Go?"

Lyle chuckled softly as he stepped toward her. "Or stay? That's up to you." When Lyle reached her, he lifted a strand of her hair and let it drift through his fingers. He didn't miss the hitch in her breath.

Taking her by the shoulders, he brought her to her feet and against him. The chair turned over with a bang but neither of them gave it any notice. His lips found hers. They were as soft and pliable and welcoming as he remembered.

There was no uncertainty on Cass's part this time. Her arms circled his neck, pulling his head closer as he took the kiss deeper. She moaned low, wiggling against him and sending his desire into orbit. Her mouth opened without his request and her tongue eagerly met his in a sensual dance.

With his desire for her increasing by the second, he buried his fingers in her hair. Cass gripped his shoulders as his mouth left hers to leave kisses along her jaw and up to her ear. She did a super-sexy wriggle against his taut length when he planted a kiss behind her ear.

Cass cupped the side of his head and guided his mouth back to hers, then kissed him deeply. His body throbbed in appreciation. Cass ran her hand over his chest and down to his belt-line. There she pulled his sweater up and his shirt out of his pants. Seconds later his skin rippled with the pleasure of her hand moving over it.

Lyle had to touch her, all of her. He lifted Cass to the back of the sofa and stepped between her legs. Finding the edge of her sweater, he stripped it from her and let it drop to the floor. He kissed her temple. "I've dreamed of doing this for so long."

"You have?" Her whispered words held a note of wonder.

He looked into her eyes. "I have."

The smile that lit her eyes and curved her mouth was suggestive and stimulating, promising delights to come. Excitement set his blood on fire.

Cass reached for his sweater and started to remove it. He stepped back just enough to whip it off. As she balanced on the sofa back, her hands went to the bottom button of his shirt. She unfastened each one with astonishing speed, pushing the material to either side, exposing his chest.

When she licked her lips, he was almost undone. Only with self-control that he wasn't aware he possessed did he manage not to flip her over on the cushions of the sofa and have his way. But Cass deserved better than that. She was someone who merited the best he could offer, and he vowed she would receive it. He cared too much about her for their joining to be anything less.

Lyle watched her face as her index finger traveled across his chest, around his nipples, then followed the line of hair disappearing beneath his pants. She let that naughty finger dip inside his waistband and tugged him to her. Her eyes were wide, questioning.

He found her lips again. When she pushed his shirt off his shoulders, he finished removing it without his mouth leaving hers. More than once he'd seen the fire in Cass. Her intensity for life was momentarily banked but he hadn't been prepared for this profound craving to explore her passion. He wanted, needed, to see more of her, touch more of her, to experience all of Cass.

Pulling her shirt up, he ran his hand over

the smoothness of her back until he found the edge of her bra and followed it around to her breast. His hand covered it. She stilled. Her breathing had turned into panting. Satisfaction filled him when just the brush of his thumb made her nipple harden, pushing against the material of the bra. He quickly found the back clasp and released the barrier. Pushing it away, he caressed her skin until he found her breasts once more. Cupping one, he judged its weight. Perfect.

Cass leaned back slightly against his arm. Her eyelids were half-closed and her lips swollen from his kisses. She was gorgeous. Stunning. Her lips parted. Heat shot through him. He pushed her shirt out of the way and covered her nipple with his mouth. Cass moaned. Her fingers ran through his hair as she held him close.

He twirled his tongue, teasing her nipple until it stood high. Cass made a crooning sound. When it turned to a coo, Lyle's heart sored. Pleased with himself, he moved to the other breast. As he achieved the same results his desire matched hers. Holding her securely around the waist with one arm, he leaned her back to view the full landscape. Cass lying out before him was beautiful scenery to behold.

Eyes satisfied, his mouth feasted on her full breasts until she forcibly pulled his lips to hers.

As her flesh meshed with his, the aching in his body became raw pain. He pulled away, helping her to sit up straight. He steadied her with his hands on her waist. "Cass, are you sure you want to do this? Do you want to go upstairs? You decide."

To his alarm and disappointment, she pulled her shirt down over the mesmerizing view. Just as he let go of her waist so she could move away she said in a soft sexy voice, "I've always wanted to see your bedroom."

Lyle grinned. "Always, is it? I like the idea of that." He offered his hand, palm up. "Then let me give you a tour."

Cass floated more than walked up the narrow stairs behind Lyle. His firm hand clasping hers reassured her of his desire. She didn't want that to ever wane.

Even so, this impulsive decision to share Lyle's bed was reckless and far out of character. Yet this newfound freedom was intensely exciting. Anticipation tingled along every nerve. Lyle's touch, his smell, the flames of desire in his eyes all drew her to him. Being with him made her feel wonderful. Made her forget her losses. Dream of the gains. She wanted these precious moments and as long as he was willing to create them, she would take all he offered.

Tomorrow she would worry about the repercussions.

Right now, she was going to enjoy feeling, being alive as never before and leave her fear and hurt outside in the cold.

Lyle's bare back was wide, solid and strong. He was everything she needed in life right now. Was she using him? Maybe, but she would see to it he received as good as he gave. Because of him she had remembered how to give and felt whole for the first time in weeks.

At the top of the stairs he turned right down a small hallway and entered a dark room. Not letting go of her hand, he continued to lead her across the floor. Her socked feet sank into a plush rug seconds before a click heralded light. A lamp sat on a small wooden table beside a large impressive bed. The dark headboard almost reached the ceiling while the matching footboard rose a few feet above the mattress. A quilt in browns and tans covered it.

Lyle turned to her. "Are you still sure you want this?"

Cass cherished his thoughtfulness. She cupped one of his cheeks. "Oh, yes." Going up on her toes, she kissed him.

That was all the invitation he seemed to require. Pulling her tight against him, Lyle tumbled with her to the bed. She winced.

Lyle said a harsh word under his breath. Raising himself so that he could see her, he asked. "Did I hurt you? I'm so sorry." He made a move to leave her.

She pulled him back. "Just a little tender. But I'm all right. How about kissing me?"

Lyle smiled. "With pleasure." His lips found hers.

As he kissed her his hands explored and caressed her waist and hips before lightly trailing between her legs. By the time they pulled apart, her center beat like a drum keeping rhythm with their heavy breathing.

Lyle rolled to his side, supported his head in his hand, and studied her. His other hand went to the hem of her shirt and beneath it. She shivered when his fingers found skin and skimmed along it. His heated gaze met hers. "Shh… I want to see all of you."

She looked away. "I have scars from the accident…"

Lyle's lips found hers briefly. "Even those. They're part of who you are now. The amazing person you are."

Cass had never thought of them like that. Her fear had been that they would be one more turn-off for men. She tried to relax as Lyle pushed her shirt and bra up, exposing her breasts. When he wanted to remove her shirt, she lifted off the bed enough for him to do so.

"More beautiful than I imagined."

She studied him in wonder. He'd been thinking about her, imagining her without clothes? The revelation was like a balm to her battered emotions.

Lyle gave her a gentle kiss before moving to one breast, then the other. "So sweet." He rotated her so he could see the injury on her arm then gently kissed the area. "I'm so sorry you were hurt."

Moments later his hand moved to the button of her pants and undid it. It took him no time to find the aching need at her center and slide a finger inside. She squirmed. Instead of giving her the relief she yearned for, his caress heightened her burning need.

"Lyle…" she crooned. Her gaze met his.

He kissed her deeply and continued his ministrations. Stopping, he tugged at her pants. Cass lifted her hips, assisting him in the process before kicking them to the floor. Lyle ran his hand along her right thigh. He paused over the puckered skin, then leaned toward it.

She shifted away. "Don't. It's so ugly."

"Shh… Nothing about you is ugly."

Lyle lightly kissed the area then his mouth moved to hers as his nimble finger entered her again. As it teased, his tongue mimicked the erotic dance.

Cass forgot everything but the sensation Lyle was creating in her. Cass's body tightened as the longing built, pleading for release. When she reached the limits of her endurance her body took over as if leaving her behind. She closed her eyes, flexed her back and tightened her legs around his hand, slipping into the land of wonder and delight that Lyle had built just for her.

Lyle's kisses gentled. He gave her one quick peck before he left her. Cass opened her eyelids just enough to see him shuck his pants in one swift movement. He stood strong and proud. Her breath caught in her throat at the beauty before her. She had caused this reaction in him. With that knowledge came a sense of amazement and power. Lyle obviously wanted her as much as she did him. He opened the drawer on the bedside table and removed a package, tore it open and rolled the condom on. Stepping to the bed, he looked down at her.

Cass opened her arms. Lyle came to her and she pulled him close. Her legs opened and he entered her slowly. She accepted all of him, but just barely. He eased out of her snug core, then plunged in again. Taking his head in both hands, Cass brought his mouth to hers. She loved kissing him. Loved how he made her feel—happy and healthy once again. Lyle increased his pace. The friction grew, building on itself. That growling need she'd known before returned with a vengeance.

Her eyes widened as she broke off their kiss and stared into Lyle's blazing ones. "Oh."

There was a lift to the corners of his mouth as she went over the edge of pleasure again.

Returning to herself, she saw the tension in Lyle's face that made his cheekbones more pronounced. His eyes were still locked with hers, but his attention was elsewhere. He thrust into her, faster and stronger. Throwing his head back, he let go a throaty groan as he found his release.

Cass's eyes slowly closed as Lyle shifted to her side, still breathing heavily. He intertwined his fingers with hers. Like their lives had become.

Could she let them remain so?

Lyle returned to bed to find Cass napping under the covers with her head on his pillow. Her scent would linger there when she was gone. Fulfillment filled his chest, made his heart light. Cass had come willingly and given without reservation.

He eased in next to her and pulled her close. She was warm and sleek along his side. After murmuring something unintelligible she settled like a kitten beside him. He brushed her hair from her face. Her lashes rested in a dark semi-circle long her cheek.

With Cass he'd found the most pleasure he'd ever experienced. He'd had relationships since Freya but only Cass had managed to capture his attention so fully that he thought of her more often than his job. No matter what he was doing, she slipped into his mind. Even after she'd left the pub this afternoon, he had been more concerned about her reaction than his own to seeing Freya.

Cass shifted against him. He looked down to find her watching him. "Hey."

A shadow of uncertainty filled her eyes. "Hi. I didn't mean to fall asleep on you."

"I'm not complaining." He hoped it would happen often. His body was already coming to life. Leaning down, he kissed her.

Cass stopped him from taking it deeper and further with a hand to his chest. "I'd better go. I don't want to miss the head count at the clinic."

Lyle wanted her to stay but he wouldn't

make her. Still, he had to protest at her leaving. "They don't do a head count, do they?"

She smirked. "So asks the man running the show."

"I'm not a dictator."

Cass sat up, bringing the sheet along to cover her. To his disappointment. Was she still self-conscious about her scars? "I know that. In fact, next to my father you're the nicest man I know."

Lyle's chest tightened. Having felt his father's disappointment most of his adult life, to hear Cass say that touched him. He felt valued. He put his hand behind her neck and brought her lips to his. "Thank you. I think that might be one of the nicest compliments I've ever received."

"You're welcome. Now I'd better get going."

By slipping off the bed and snatching up her clothes, she gave him no time to argue. "Bathroom?"

Lyle gave a fleeting thought to outright asking her to stay. He didn't. Apparently she needed distance to think about what had just happened between them. Maybe he wanted that as well. He pointed. "Door in the hall."

When he heard the door close, he got up, dressed and went downstairs. Cass didn't even come into the living room where he was. Instead she went straight to her boots. It was as if she was running. Was she regretting what had happened?

She was in the process of pulling on her jacket when he placed his hands on her shoulders. "Cass."

"Yes?"

"What's going on inside that head of yours?"

She didn't look up.

Suppressing a sigh of frustration, he said, "I think we've come far enough in our relationship that we can trust each other. Why the speedy exit? At this rate you're starting to put a dent in my self-confidence."

That brought her head up. "Oh, no. It has nothing to do with you. It has everything to do with me. I don't want the staff gossiping about us. But let me assure you your ego is well deserved."

He wanted to thump his chest but he settled for a big smile. "That's good to hear. I'll walk you back to the castle." He helped her on with her jacket then pulled on his coat.

Outside the cottage Lyle took her hand. He was relieved Cass didn't try to pull free, half-afraid she would.

At the side door of the castle, she held him back when he would have gone in. "It might be a good idea for us to say goodnight here.

Do you really want the staff to know the despicable things you've been doing to a resident?"

Lyle chuckled. "Despicable? What about the wicked things you did to me?"

"Wicked?" She sounded appalled.

"I like the wicked you. But I agree. We should keep this between us. There's no reason we should be the talk of the clinic, or the village for that matter." She already had enough troubling her. He didn't want her worrying about gossip.

Cass reached for the doorknob.

"You're forgetting something." Lyle brought her to him and kissed her soundly. They broke apart and he searched her face. "Sometime soon I plan to have you to myself all night."

Cass's eyes widened, as her mouth opened and closed before she shut the door between them.

Gratification filled him. She was not as unaffected by what had taken place between them as she acted.

CHAPTER SEVEN

TWO DAYS LATER Cass sat in the castle lounge in front of the roaring fire snuggled into one of the wing-backed chairs. She was attempting to read a book she'd found in the library about the history of Cluchlochry. What she was really doing was thinking about Lyle. She had only spoken to him briefly a couple of times since they had been together. He acted as if he was abiding by her implied suggestion they make their time in bed together a one-time occurrence. Even though she had intentionally given that impression, she missed kissing him or being held in his arms. It was driving her crazy not seeing him. But she would be leaving soon. Could her heart stand for her to take it further?

Was he waiting for her to come to him? Could she let herself do that? Would she be able not to? Indecision roiled in her.

It was a relief to have the distraction when

Melissa pushed a young man in a wheelchair into the room and over beside her. At least now she had something to take her mind off Lyle.

The young man, dressed in a T-shirt and sweatpants, looked older than she guessed was the reality. He was gaunt. Dark rings beneath his eyes emphasized his lost look. One of his hands had a tremor.

"Hi, Cass. Have you met Andy Wallace?" Melissa asked as she parked the man near the fire. A small brown and white cocker spaniel jogged along beside him, coming to lie at his feet.

"No, I haven't. Hi, Andy." A week ago, could she have sounded that friendly? Being at the castle had changed her...or had it been Lyle? The thought both worried and thrilled her.

Andy nodded, then looked down at his clasped hands in his lap.

Wasn't he the patient who had been admitted the same day as she had been? In all the time she'd been there she hadn't seen him. "I've heard of you. Nice to meet you."

Melissa locked the brake on the wheelchair. She patted him on the shoulder. "I need to check on another patient then I'll be back to take you to therapy. I won't be long."

She gave Cass a quick smile and was gone.

Andy's eyes flickered to Cass with a look of uncertainty before they jerked away.

She leaned down and patted the dog. Not long ago she wouldn't have done that. "I do know Molasses. I work at the canine therapy center every afternoon so I get to take care of Molasses when she isn't with you. She's a good dog."

"Maybe when I start walking I can do that as well. The doctors keep telling me I'll walk again but I'm not sure that'll ever happen."

"Getting well takes time. I'm sure you'll get there." Who did she think she was to give encouragement when she'd been little more than a walking package of ugly emotions with a bad leg and arm a couple of weeks ago? This morning she'd even caught herself smiling when she thought of Lyle. Her leg was getting stronger and her arm was extending further. She smiled. Lyle had kissed her injuries. She had made more progress than she could have believed possible when she had arrived. For once she'd started thinking there was a future.

Andy said nothing more as he stared into the fire.

There wouldn't be much conversation unless she helped keep it going. She sensed he needed it. Wasn't that what Lyle had seen in her? The need to talk about the unseen trauma that physical therapy had no effect on? Could she help do for Andy what Lyle had done for her? Giving him an ear, just listen to him?

She raised the book in her hand. "I've been reading about the history of Cluchlochry. This is an amazing area."

He grunted.

A response. Somewhat.

"We don't have anything like this where I'm from." She waved a hand indicating the castle. "It's a special place."

"I used to spend a lot of time here," he muttered.

Cass had to lean forward to hear him. There was moisture pooling in his eyes.

"You've been to Heatherglen Castle before?"

"Yes. I grew up in Cluchlochry." His voice had grown stronger.

"It must have been a fun place for little boys. There are plenty of places to hide. Big spaces to run." The castle and grounds would be a wonderful place to spend a childhood. Would Lyle's kids one day do that? The thought of him having children with another woman caused a dull ache around her heart.

Andy's eyes took on a shadowed look. "Nick and I used to play hide and seek here all the time. I never could find him." He didn't say anything more, returning to staring at the fire. "He's gone now."

"Gone?" she prompted.

"Died in Afghanistan."

Cass sucked in a breath.

"Nick was my best friend," he mumbled.

She wasn't sure who he was talking about, but the name sounded familiar. Waiting, she hoped he'd answer her questions without her saying more.

"It should have been me who died. He should have got out of the army. Should have come home. Not gone back. I told him not to," he said, less to her and more to himself.

Cass's heart went out to him. She cringed, too well acquainted with loss. Of emotions so enormous and distressing they were difficult to live with. Hers had many fronts. Rufus being gone. What to do with her life now. Could she have a real lasting relationship with a man? Now to live with the scars. All of those were bundled into a massive ball of insecurity. She could understand the forlorn man beside her too well. That added to her discomfort. "Heatherglen was Nick's home?"

Andy gave her an odd look as if he was confused by her confusion. "Nick was Charles's older brother. Dr. Charles Ross-Wylde, the Laird."

"Yes, I've met the Laird. I know who you're talking about now. I'm sorry to hear about your friend. Losing someone you care about is hard."

"Have you lost someone?"

This was not the direction Cass had anticipated their conversation going. If she had she wouldn't have started it. Over the last few days thoughts of Lyle had managed to overtake all those ugly, sad feelings that had weighed heavy on her and she liked it that way. The pain had dulled. Maybe, just maybe, if she could share some of her pain with Andy, he wouldn't feel so alone, maybe believe that life could get better.

To her surprise, she had begun to believe that. It had slipped up on her but, yes, she did. "I have. It wasn't a person but the next thing to it. He was my partner and friend. Rufus, my dog."

Andy gave her a long searching look. "What happened?"

Cass wasn't sure she could go into the details but she'd opened the door so Andy deserved the truth. Her eyes clouded over. "We were a search and rescue team. We had just saved a child when there was a ground tremor and the wall of the building started to fall. Rufus barked, warning me. The wall fell on

him. Hit me in the leg and arm." She could say
this next part. Had to say it. "He saved my life
and lost his."

Andy gave her a compassionate look. "I'm
sorry about your dog."

Moisture filled Cass's eyes, making Andy
a foggy blur. "I miss him every day. I'm not
sure if I can or want to return to my job without him. It may be just too hard. But search
and rescue is all I know."

Lyle walked to the lounge door when he heard
Cass's voice. He halted inside the door, just in
time to hear her confession about Rufus. He
listened for more. She hadn't told him the entire story. No wonder she had been so devas-
tated by what had happened to her. The loss of
the dog was some of it but her fears and agony
went deeper. Her world had been turned upside
down. She was unsure what direction to take.
The change in her life must be terrifying for
her. She'd experienced a major loss of not only
her dog but life as she had known it. He knew
her well enough to know that, for her, losing
her job was like losing her identity.

Yet she had shared her grief and feelings
with another hurting person. That had to have
been difficult for her. He should feel hurt that
she had confided the deeper meaning of the

loss of Rufus with Andy and not him, but what Lyle had just heard told him what a large heart Cass had for people.

Andy had refused to come out of his room for days. Lyle had finally convinced him to come down. On top of not wanting to interact with others, Andy refused to talk about his accident and about losing Nick. Lyle would be eternally grateful to Cass for getting him to open up, to take a metaphorical step forward.

Cass and Andy were so adsorbed in their conversation they didn't see or hear him. He shouldn't stand here eavesdropping but he couldn't move either. Thankfully that was taken out of his hands when Melissa brushed past him.

"Hi, Lyle. How're you today?" She kept going until she reached Andy.

Cass's head whipped around so that she looked directly at him. Surprise, concern and happiness ran over her features in rapid progression.

Lyle was glad to see her as well, but he was still disturbed by what he had heard and what it meant in her life. He had made less of it in his mind than he should have. He now understood why Cass acted the way she did about the dog they'd found, the sadness about her when she'd first arrived, even her not wanting to get too involved with him. Her emotions must be in turmoil. She had been and was suffering far more than he'd given her credit for.

He stepped forward as Melissa announced as she took off the brake on the chair, "They're waiting for you in therapy, Andy. We must go."

Andy gave Cass a nod.

She offered him a wry smile. "See you soon, Andy."

Melissa rolled him back, turned him and they headed out the door.

Cass's eyes rose to meet Lyle's. "You heard?"

Lyle nodded. He didn't even try to question why she hadn't shared with him how losing Rufus had affected her. Now wasn't the time to analyze that. There might never be one. She didn't owe him anything. One hot evening together didn't mean they could or should bare their souls to one another. That was the way she seemed to want it. Didn't he as well?

Pushing herself to her feet, she said, "I'd better go."

He took a couple of steps forward, his voice going low. "I've missed you, Cass. I was coming to look for you when I heard your voice."

"Did you want something?"

"I'd like a kiss." He looked around, "But I won't do that here."

Cass rewarded him with a blush. She might

be acting as if she was immune to him but she wasn't, not even a little bit.

"I'll wait until later. But I will kiss you." He stressed the last sentence.

She grinned at him. "Is that a promise, Doctor?"

Lyle's heart soared. He liked that much better than her sad look. "It is. I do have something to ask you, though. My mother rang and would like me to bring you around to Harlow House for dinner this evening. She wants to keep her promise to teach you to knit."

Cass looked away as if she was unsure. "That's not necessary."

He waited until she met his gaze again. "My mother will be disappointed if you don't come."

Cass looked down as if her shoes required her attention. "I'm just not sure that's a good idea."

"Why not? You have been invited." Lyle watched her closely. It shouldn't matter so much that she agree.

"I don't want to give her any ideas about us, with me leaving so soon."

"If that's now you feel..." He turned to go.

She reached out and grabbed his forearm. "Wait."

Lyle didn't realize until that second just how

much he'd missed Cass's touch. He placed his hand over hers.

Cass's eyelids fluttered as she gave him a wary look. "I guess I could go. I'd never want to hurt your mother's feelings."

He made a *tsk*ing sound. "And here I was hoping you wanted to spend time with me. I'll meet you in the foyer at five."

She nodded.

Lyle ran his thumb across the top of her hand. "By the way, Cass, you're beautiful both inside and out. You really helped Andy out today. He needs someone to confide in, someone who understands where he's coming from. You're a special person, Cass Bellow."

Her eyes softened. Lyle had to leave before he kissed her right then and there.

A few hours later Lyle strolled into the foyer, expecting to see Cass waiting near the door. Instead he found her with a staff member and a couple of other residents, tying large red bows on the banister. The greenery had been draped the week before.

"It's really starting to look like Christmas in here." His attention was directly on Cass.

Everyone turned to him.

"Thank you," the staff member said. "I have some excellent help."

"I have one more bow to tie and I'll be ready," Cass called.

There was a happy note in her voice. That had been missing when she'd first arrived and he rather liked hearing it. Had he had anything to do with putting it there? He really hoped so. "We have time."

She moved up a step with only a slight hesitation. Soon she would be coming down those stairs as part of her graduation and be leaving him. The thought brought a wince deep within him. Did he want her to stay? Could he ask her to? He refused to do a long-distance relationship again. From experience he'd learned those didn't work. Cass's life was going all over the world, helping people, and his was staying here and doing the same. It would never work. It would be better for both of them to let go sooner than later.

Another few minutes went by before Cass came down the steps slowly, holding tightly to the rail, but she was doing it on her own. She approached him.

"You have made progress. It won't be long before you'll be going up and coming down the grand staircase instead of using the lift."

She smiled and his world brightened. "I have to admit that a few weeks ago I looked at it as if it was Mount Everest. I was halfway up before I knew it."

"You've worked hard. You should be proud of yourself." Lyle was.

"Thanks." Cass picked up her coat off a chair and slipped into it. Buttoning it, she quickly wrapped the scarf around her neck and pulled on her hat.

"Ready?"

"I am." She headed toward the front door.

Lyle followed. When they were out of hearing of the others he asked, "I thought you didn't want anyone to know about our...uh, friendship? You didn't seem to mind the others knowing you were going out with me."

Over her shoulder she said, "I told them you were testing my endurance by going for a walk with me."

"Ah, I see." He had a sour taste in his mouth. When she had suggested the other night that they keep their relationship between themselves it'd seemed the wise thing to do. Now he wanted people to know that Cass was his and he hers. Or was it really that way? "We do need to walk to my place and then take the car from there."

"Your parents live far?" She started around the castle toward the path to his cottage.

"No, but further than *you* would even wish to walk."

They were soon out of sight of the castle and Lyle took her hand. His heart thumped an extra beat when she didn't pull away. After they reached the seclusion of the large trees, he pulled her behind one and into his arms.

"I've waited too long to do this." His lips found hers.

Unsure what Cass's reaction would be, he was elated when she stepped into him and joined him in a kiss that should have melted the snow beneath their feet. They stayed like that until the wind blew and a pile of snow dropped off a branch, landing on their shoulders. They giggled like school kids then started toward his place again.

Once there, Lyle led her to the detached garage to where he kept his car. Inside it, he reached over and cupped her cheek. "I have missed you. I wished there was time to take you inside and have my way with you, but my mother is expecting us."

Cass smiled. "We all like to keep our parents happy."

He groaned. "That we do." He'd spent the better part of his life trying to do just that and was still managing to disappoint his father. If he returned to the army, he would be choosing his father's happiness over his own.

Cass looked over at Lyle as he backed out of the garage. It had been so long since she had been alone with him that she'd feared she might rush into his arms when she did have him to herself. The moment she had looked up from tying the bow to the spindle and her gaze had locked with his, her heart had galloped like a horse making the last quarter-mile.

What had he been thinking? Had he been as excited to see her? She'd left things between them as if their time together had been nothing but a nice evening. She'd been fooling herself. Being with Lyle had been more than that. She couldn't say that to him earlier in the lounge, so she was glad to have the invitation to his parents'. They would have a chance to talk. More than that, to touch.

She'd only agreed to help decorate the foyer because it gave her nervous energy an outlet. If she hadn't, she would have been pacing the floor when he arrived. It had to have been high school since she'd last been this wired up about seeing a guy. Her attraction to Lyle had tipped over into need in such a short time.

That horse had broken into an even faster gallop the second Lyle had pulled her out of sight of the castle and kissed her. She'd been back where she belonged. When the snow had fallen on them she had laughed like she hadn't laughed in far too long. Instead of having second thoughts about becoming involved with Lyle, she was running headlong into doing so. Especially by going to his parents' house.

After Lyle had driven onto the main road, he took her hand and held it as often as the narrow winding roads would allow. He drove through the village and out the other side. Soon he turned into a lane that led to a stately house that was a larger version of Lyle's cottage.

Lyle's mother greeted her by pulling her into a hug. Cass instantly missed her own mother, who she hoped to see soon. She glanced at Lyle. That would mean she would be leaving him. At that moment, she decided she would make the most of the time she had with him. She wanted this happiness to last as long as possible. The difference between misery and joy had been made clear over the last couple of weeks and she would take all the cheer in life she could grab for as long as she could have it. Right now, that meant being with Lyle.

When Mrs. Sinclair finished embracing Cass, she moved on to Lyle with the same vigor, as if she hadn't seen him in years. Done, she escorted them into a living area where the

TV was on. Lyle's father didn't stand as they entered.

Mr. Sinclair did offer his hand. "Hello again, young lady."

Lyle would age well based on his father's looks, despite the older man's illness. Some other woman would get to watch that. Cass wasn't going to think of that now. "Hello. Thanks for having me."

"Glad to. Hello, son." He and Lyle shook hands.

Something about the action bothered Cass. Shouldn't they have hugged? A second of coolness seemed to surround them.

"Cass and I are going to the kitchen to have our knitting lesson," Mrs. Sinclair announced, and turned to Cass. "Unless you have changed your mind?"

"Oh, no, I would love to learn."

"Then come with me. Lyle, you watch the match with your dad while we have our lesson." Mrs. Sinclair waved a hand at him as she moved toward a door off the room.

Cass glanced at Lyle who was already settling into a chair. Maybe Cass had just been imagining things. Lyle acted as if spending time with his father wasn't a problem.

She found the more she was around Lyle's parents the more she liked them. His mother was what every mother should be—warm and open. His father was harder to get to know with his gruff voice and iron exterior, but Cass suspected he loved his wife and son deeply, and they him.

Cass followed Mrs. Sinclair into the kitchen. It, like the rest of the house, was in perfect order. The counter tops were spotless and the floor gleamed.

"Why don't we sit by the fire? We'll be warm there."

A large range sat against one wall with two rocking chairs in front of it. Beside one of the chairs was a basket full of yarn with large needles stuck in it.

Cass took the chair that didn't have the basket next to it, reasoning that it was Mrs. Sinclair's.

Lyle's mother settled into the other. "We're going to start with something simple. Just learn to knit. I think it will be all that you want to do in the first lesson. Now I'm going to show you how to start then I'm going to let you do it."

Cass eagerly sat on the edge of her seat, watching every move Mrs. Sinclair made. "That sounds fine. I know nothing about knitting."

Mrs. Sinclair's mouth formed a smile much

like Lyle's. "Today you'll learn. Here are some needles and you pick out a skein of wool."

"They're all so lovely." Cass decided on a blue that reminded her of the color of Lyle's eyes. When she was gone at least she would have that to remember him by.

Lyle's mother picked up some needles and pulled out a length of wool. "The first thing you want to do is make a small loop and slide it onto one of the needles."

Mrs. Sinclair was already in her element. Cass watched intently.

"Now you bring this up around here, the tip of the needle through here and the wool around like this." The wool worked perfectly onto the needle. "Now I want you to try with your needles and wool."

Cass did as she had been shown until it was time to move the wool up and around the needle.

"Not quite, dear." Mrs. Sinclair's voice was patient. Did Lyle get that from her as well? "Let me show you." She brought the wool around and got Cass started correctly once again.

Cass had made ten rows and was proud of her accomplishment when Lyle's voice came from behind her. "It looks like you're making progress."

Cass held up what she had done. "Look, I'm actually knitting."

He smiled as if he was proud of her as well.

"She's a really good student," Mrs. Sinclair offered.

"Cass is good at anything she puts her mind to," Lyle said.

A warmth that had nothing to do with the fire spread through her. Looking over her shoulder again, Cass saw Lyle gazing at her with a twinkle in his eye. Was he thinking about their time together in bed? She gave him a shy smile then glanced at his mother to find her watching them closely. Did she see the attraction between them?

"I hate to break this up, but Dad and I were wondering how long it would be until dinner?"

Mrs. Sinclair put her work into her basket and stood. "Lyle Sinclair, you know as well as anyone that in this house we eat promptly at six. We have all your life. Gregor wouldn't have it any other way."

"Yes, once in the army always in the army." Lyle said it as fact, but there was a note of bitterness there as well.

She gave her son a direct look. "I'll have you know I don't worry about you starving when you eat Mrs. Renwick's food all the time."

Lyle's mood lightened. "I do have to be careful not to overdo it there."

Cass placed her work in the basket as well. "What can I do to help?"

"We're just having a chicken pie tonight. It's already in the oven so there's not much to do except set the table."

"Lyle and I can take care of that, can't we?" Cass looked at him.

An amazed look came to his face, but he nodded. "Yes, we can."

Over the next few minutes she and Lyle gathered what was needed. A couple of times he brushed past her, making her tingle all over. When she asked him for a fork he handed it across the table in a manner that let him trail his fingers over her palm, which started her center throbbing. She'd had no idea that setting the table could be such an erotic activity. Her eyes met his. She didn't see a flicker of desire there, but a fire burning.

His mother cleared her throat, bringing them back to where they were. Cass dropped the fork with a clang onto a plate.

Lyle, the devil, grinned and picked it up. He put it in its place. "All done, Mum."

His mother smiled. "Thank you." She turned back to the counter to where a large bowl sat.

"Oh, my goodness, we all need to give the pudding a stir. I don't want to forget it."

"Pudding a stir?" Cass gave the bowl a dubious look. "Exactly what're we doing?"

"Stirring the Christmas pudding," Mrs. Sinclair stated, as if it was a great occasion.

"I don't know what a Christmas pudding is." Cass looked into the bowl from which she had removed the cloth.

"I think they call it a fruit cake in America." Lyle moved up beside Cass.

"I have heard of them but never seen one or eaten one." Cass still studied the mixture.

"You'll have to join us for some in a few weeks." Lyle's mother pulled out a large wooden spoon from a drawer.

Cass felt more than saw Lyle tense beside her. Did it matter to him that she would be gone soon? It did her. She wanted as much time with him as possible before she left. "I'm not sure that I'll be here that long."

"Well, if you're here then you must come for a slice." Mrs. Sinclair didn't miss a beat. "You need to stir three times and then make a wish."

Lyle's mother handed her the spoon.

Wish? What should she wish for? To hurry home? For a new partner? She wasn't sure she was ready for that. She glanced at Lyle. To have him in her life always? What did she want most? Happiness. She glanced at Lyle. She felt that right now. But could it last?

It took more effort than she'd anticipated to stir the thick mixture but she managed to make the three turns. She made her wish.

"So what did you ask for?" Lyle took the spoon and started to stir.

"I can't tell you that. It won't come true." And she wanted it to come true no matter how improbable and unrealistic it was.

His mother stepped away. Lyle whispered, "Was it about me?"

Cass whispered back, "Such an ego."

"Lyle, if you'll carry the pie to the table and Cass brings the beans, I think we'll be ready." Mrs. Sinclair pulled a round golden-brown-crusted pie out of the oven. It smelled heavenly. She set it on the counter.

Lyle then picked it up and moved it to the table. His mother handed her the bowl with beans in it.

"Gregor," Mrs. Sinclair called. "Come to the table."

Lyle's father joined them, but it took him a while. He moved slowly.

Over the next hour they enjoyed good food and lively conversation. Cass looked around the cozy room. At Lyle. This was what she would like to have in her life. Lyle smiled at her. This was happiness.

"So what do you do in America?" Lyle's father asked her.

Her heart sank at the reminder. This wasn't her home. "I work in search and rescue." Did she still, though?

Gregor nodded. "Interesting work."

"It can be." She didn't really want to talk about it. "I understand you're retired military?"

He sat straighter, if that was possible. "I am. All the men in my family have made a career in the armed forces." He gave Lyle, who had turned stony-faced, a pointed look. "I'm hoping Lyle will decide to go active again soon."

She looked at Lyle, who was pushing food around on his plate. Had she said something wrong?

"Dad, let's not get into that now."

For the first time since Cass had arrived Mrs. Sinclair had no smile on her face. An uncomfortable feeling settled around them, completely wiping out the ease of earlier.

She had said something wrong!

Lyle's request went unnoticed by Mr. Sinclair. "You need to do it soon or time will run out for promotions."

"Isn't Lyle needed here? You should have

seen him in action the other night. He had
two patients to see about and then me. I understand that he's the only emergency medical care around here. That's a big burden for
anyone. I think there are different ways of
fighting for people. You did it by being in the
military and Lyle does it by caring for people
when they are hurt. In my book you're both
heroes."

The others looked at her, speechless. Not
even Mr. Sinclair said a thing. Lyle gave her a
tender look of wonderment and appreciation.

Mrs. Sinclair pushed back from the table.
"I'll get those biscuits I bought at the market
the other day for dessert."

An hour later Lyle was driving them back to
his cottage.

"I hope I didn't say anything wrong at dinner," Cass said in a small voice. "I didn't mean
to."

Lyle couldn't believe that Cass had even
asked that. After her speech to his father Lyle's
chest had puffed out like a bird preening for
a new mate. Few managed to put his father
in his place and Cass had done it effortlessly
and had complimented his father at the same
time. Lyle looked at her like she was a queen.

"You were wonderful. The subject is an age-old sticky issue between my father and me."

"How's that?" Her attention was focused on him.

"You could tell that I'm a disappointment to him. He's sick. Dying, in fact."

Cass squeezed the hand he already held. "I'm sorry."

"I am, too. If I re-enlisted he'd be so happy. I could give him that before he died. Right now, I'm letting the family name down."

"You are not! He can't believe that. You help people. Look how much you have helped me."

Lyle raised a brow and gave her a suggestive look. "I don't help all the residents in the same way as I have you."

Her lips turned up in a smirk and she poked him in the shoulder with a finger. "And you had better not."

He was even feeling better about himself after that statement. It was the first time Cass had indicated that she felt any ownership of him, that he was important to her on a level outside bed. He liked the idea of her being jealous. She was definitely good for his ego.

Lyle pulled into his garage and turned off the engine. Twisting toward Cass he brought her to him. She looked at him expectantly. "I thought you were perfect tonight. Thank you for the vote of confidence. It means a lot. Especially coming from you."

Cass gave him a tender smile as his lips slowly lowered to hers. They were as soft as he remembered. A second later, her hands gripped his coat and pulled him closer. She returned his kiss. He lifted her onto his lap. It wasn't until she winced that he remembered her injuries.

He let go of her and she slid back into the passenger seat. "I'm sorry again. I keep forgetting you've been hurt. That hero certificate you said I deserved should be revoked."

"I'm fine. When I make certain moves my leg lets me know it doesn't like it."

"Necking in a two-seater car would be one of those times." What was wrong with him? He forgot everything but touching Cass when she was near. He climbed out of the car and hurried around to help her out. "I'm really sorry."

She wrapped her finger around his coat lapels and pulled him to her again. "Why don't you shut up and kiss me, then take me inside?"

He brought her into his arms with a smile on his lips. "I can do that."

CHAPTER EIGHT

FOUR MORNINGS LATER Cass was still in his bed when he woke up. Lyle liked it that way. Too much. She had stayed the night after they had gone to his parents'. They had agreed to eating dinner at his place the next evening.

As he'd held her in his arms after they had made love, he'd asked, "Will you stay the night?"

She'd leaned up to look at him. "I will if you understand that this can only be a short-term thing between us. As soon as I am given a clean bill of health, I'm going home. I can't handle anything serious in my life right now. I've just gotten to where I can get out of bed without dreading it."

Lyle had wiggled his brows. "That wouldn't be because you've been in bed with me, would it?"

She'd brushed a hand low over him and his body had twitched in reaction. "You might say that. I just need things to remain easy and fun between us. I've been on emotional overload for so long. I don't think I could handle more."

"I can do slow and easy. In fact, I'd like to practice now." He'd rolled Cass on her side and brushed a feather-light finger over her hip. Lyle had been rewarded with a shiver from Cass.

The next two nights they had eaten at the castle and then walked hand in hand to his place. Lyle had tried not to question Cass's decisions. Instead, he enjoyed having her in his life. No one at the castle had asked him where she was at night and he'd offered no explanation. All he knew was that life was better than it had ever been.

What they didn't do was talk about when she was leaving. Yet both knew it was coming. Too fast for him. Did Cass feel the same way? He didn't want to ruin what they had by asking.

On Saturday morning, they were lying in bed and Cass's hand was causally rubbing back and forth over his chest when she asked, "Hey, have you ever thought about making this place more festive? Everyone else is busy decorating for Christmas but you have nothing up."

"Are you thinking I should have a tree in my bedroom?"

Her hand gave him a light swat. Which he liked more than resented. "Of course not. I was thinking of you putting one up in your living room. It looks like Scrooge lives here."

"You can hurt my feelings, you know? I'd just planned to enjoy what's up at the castle. I've never really gone in for that sort of stuff, and I go to Mum and Dad's on Christmas Day." He pushed her hair back, letting his fingers run through it. "But maybe if I had somebody to help me, I could put a few things up. Would you be willing to help?"

Cass twisted around, looking him in the face while giving him a tantalizing view of the curve of her breast and hip. She seemed to give no thought to having scars anymore. "I thought you would never ask."

Lyle chuckled.

She grinned. "So do you have any ornaments or anything to put on a tree?"

"No. I hadn't had any need for them."

"Then we'll go to the Christmas market and get some. I saw some really pretty ones made out of natural stuff in one of the stalls."

Later Cass sat at the kitchen table, having a cup of coffee, while he scrambled eggs and prepared toast. She looked up and smiled. Lyle liked this Cass much better than the one who had first arrived at the castle. He would miss her when she was gone. "I really appreciate you talking to Andy. I've been worried about him."

"Unfortunately, I think we have a lot in common." There was a dejected note in her words.

"You might be right about that." He really couldn't break patient confidentiality. "I wish you hadn't kept all that happened to you from me, but I understand why you did. I'm so sorry."

She gave him a look of appreciation then went back to her coffee. Cass would talk more when she was ready. He finished the eggs, put the toast on a plate and carried it all to the table.

"I can help you." Cass reached for the plate.

"I told you that I wanted to cook for you. If we're going to get a tree and ornaments today you need to keep up your strength." He winked. "I might have other plans for you as well."

He was rewarded with an attractive blush. She never stopped amazing him. Cass was as tough as stone on the outside but could blush like a young woman after her first kiss. He loved the two sides of her. Love! Was he falling in love with Cass?

She spooned out scrambled eggs and took a piece of toast. "So can we go to the market as soon as we're through eating?"

"Are we in that much of a hurry?"

Cass gave him an insistent look. "We have a

lot to do if we're going to get this place looking festive today."

"We have to do it all today?" He gave a theatrical groan.

She put her fists on her hips and gave him a huffy look. "We do. I won't be here much longer, and I want to enjoy it for as long as I can."

That statement stabbed Lyle with reality, but he refused to let on that her leaving would upset him. She wanted casual and he would try to give her that. He chuckled. "Where did all this newfound Christmas spirit come from?"

Cass looked directly into his eyes. "From being around you. Thank you for bringing me back from that dark place."

His heart swelled. This was what it was like to be appreciated, valued for who he was as a person. He'd not felt that in some time. He needed it. Cass had given him a real gift. "You're welcome." He kissed her, keeping it tender, wanting her to sense his gratitude, then he pulled away, "You're right, I do need some cheer."

Soon after they'd finished breakfast, they left for the village. Few people were around. The sky was dark and it was starting to spit. It would snow again before the end of the day. Cass led the way to the stall with the ornaments she had seen. There, the owner greeted Lyle, whom he had known all his life.

Lyle told Cass, "Get whatever you think I need."

She grinned. "You shouldn't have said that." Cass went about picking out ornaments and putting them into a pile on the corner of the table.

Lyle paid the man, who was grinning from ear to ear as they walked off.

"Shouldn't we stop and say hi to your mother?" Cass looped her hand in the crook of his elbow.

"Yes. She would be hurt to know you came here and didn't say hello." Lyle led her down another aisle to his mother's stall.

His mother saw them and stopped knitting to greet them. "What're you two doing here?"

Cass gave this mother a self-satisfied smile and held up the bag she carried. "We came to get some ornaments for Lyle's tree."

His mother gave him a pointed look then asked with a sarcastic note, "Lyle's going to have a tree?"

He'd not had a tree or decorated his cottage since his return home. Freya had always made a big deal out of Christmas but he had never cared one way or the other. It wasn't worth the effort as far as he was concerned. But if Cass wanted him to have a tree, he would have a tree with all the trimmings.

"He is," Cass said proudly.

His mother looked from him to her and back again. Her smile had broadened.

"We're on our way to get one right now but we wanted to come by and say hi to you." The cheerful words seemed to bubble out of her.

"Gregor," his mother called.

Lyle turned to see his father shuffling toward them. He looked more tired than usual, older.

"Hello, son. I'm glad I got to see you. I spoke to Colonel McWright a minute ago. He said you haven't been by to talk to him about re-enlisting."

That was the last conversation Lyle wanted to have with him. "I've been busy at the clinic. I'll try to get by sometime this week."

"You need to do so. He'll be retiring soon and won't have the influence he has now. If you want that position you need to be talking to him."

The smile on Cass's face faded to an expression of curiosity and concern. Lyle wanted that smile to return. His hand went to Cass's elbow. "I'll take care of it. It's good to see you. Cass and I are putting up a tree so we need to go and pick out one before they're all gone." He started them toward the door.

"Nice to see you, Colonel and Mrs. Sinclair." Cass waved.

"Bye, Mum. Dad," Lyle called as they walked away.

Cass pulled to a halt when they were out of sight of his parents. "Are you really returning to active duty?"

"No. Maybe. I don't know. Look, we have a fun day planned and I don't want to talk about that. Let's concentrate on putting up a tree."

Cass studied him a moment then smiled brightly. "Works for me."

He would miss that smile when she returned to America. A stab of pain shot through him. This wasn't supposed to happen. He didn't, wouldn't, do long distance. It didn't work. He'd learned that the hard way. Yet he couldn't stop himself from holding onto what time he had left with her.

Cass came to another sudden stop at a stall selling Christmas-tree skirts. She fingered a navy one with silver stars sewn closer to the trunk of the tree and sloping mounds of white depicting snowy mountains. Was she think-ing of the night he had found her sitting on the rock wall? Lyle smiled. Even then he had been captivated by her.

"Get it, if you want it." He pulled out his wallet.

"I wasn't asking you to buy it." She gave him a concerned look.

He gave her an indulgent smile. "I know that, but every good tree needs a skirt."

A few minutes later they left. Cass carried their purchases with a happy look on her face.

On their way back to his cottage they stopped at a place on the outskirts of the village to buy a tree. He had to remind Cass that his ceilings weren't that high when she admired a ten-foot tree. With an exaggerated expression of disappointment, she located a six-foot tree that he still hoped would fit through his doors. Cass's happiness with her choice made him keep his concerns to himself.

They made one more stop at a shop and bought a tree stand and lights. They spent the remainder of the day putting up the Christmas tree and decorating it. Done, they switched off the main lights and sat by the fire with a hot cup of tea.

Cass laid her head on his shoulder. "What kinds of family Christmas traditions does your family have?"

"You already know about the Christmas

pudding. One year when I was off on the other side of the world Mum posted one to me. I hate to admit I was pretty lonely that year."

Cass said softly, "It was the year you got the letter."

For once the mention of what had happened to him didn't include pain. "It was. I sliced the pudding and shared it with the patients in my unit and we had a right fine celebration."

Lyle looked at Cass. To his amazement she had tears in her eyes. "What's all this about?"

She took his hand and tenderly rubbed it. "I just hate to think of you away by yourself at Christmas."

"Aw, honey, I'm home now. My Christmases are happy. This one will be especially so with this tree." What he didn't say was that he wished she would be there as well. He wouldn't think about that; instead he would enjoy what he had at this moment. She would be leaving soon. They had an agreement. Still the need to keep her there pulled at him.

A heavy knock at the front door broke the moment. Lyle opened it to find one of the local police officers standing there.

"Lyle, a five-year-old girl has gone missing. She wandered off from the market. We need your help to search."

"Missing?" The low sound of Cass's voice held a looming note of fear.

He forced himself to concentrate on what the policeman was saying. Cass he would soothe later. "How long has she been gone?"

"Two and a half hours." The policeman was wasting no time in giving answers.

His next question made him sick to ask but it was necessary. "Do you believe someone has taken her?"

The man's lips thinned. "Right now, no, but we're ruling out no possibilities."

"What do I need to do?"

"We've made a grid of the area." He handed him a map. "We need you to look here." He pointed to a square.

Cass came to stand in front of Lyle. "Do you have a piece of the child's clothing?" she asked in a determined voice. "I can help."

"You are?"

"This is Cass Bellow. She's trained in search and rescue," Lyle offered.

Cass let him say no more. "Time's of the essence. Do you have something or not?"

The officer glanced at Lyle. He nodded. "I can get something."

"Then we'll meet you at the market cross in twenty minutes." She made that announcement, turned and started putting on her coat.

"We'll see you then," Lyle said.

The officer looked unsure, but nodded and left.

Lyle closed the door and asked Cass, "What're you thinking?"

"One of the dogs at the center has past search and rescue training. I've been working with him. He knows me. He might be able to help." She wrapped her scarf around her neck.

Lyle had to admire her. Working with a dog on a search had to take all her fortitude. For her to even volunteer said something about what kind of person she was. "You sure you can handle that?"

"Don't really have a choice. A child is missing." She jerked her hat down around her ears and opened the door.

"Hey, wait for me." Lyle snatched up his scarf and hat and hurried after her.

CHAPTER NINE

"KOMM!" CASS COMMANDED Hero out of his pen at the canine center. She had made friends with him over the past couple of weeks so she had no trouble encouraging him to come to her. As he exited the cage she clipped on the leash. *"Fuss."* Hero walked beside her to Lyle's car.

He opened the door and Cass said, *"Komm,"* and Hero jumped into the backseat.

Less than a minute later they were on their way into Cluchlochry.

Cass clutched her hands in her lap. It hadn't been long since she'd had an assignment and worked with a dog, yet it seemed like years. She was a bundle of nerves. What if she broke down? What if they couldn't find the girl? What if…? All that fear and sadness that had held her heart in a vise had returned. If Rufus was here she'd have no doubts about locating the girl but she didn't know Hero well or his abilities. Still, she had to try.

Lyle drove faster than the speed limit, but every minute mattered. Hero sat calmly in the backseat of the car. Lyle pulled into a parking space close to the market cross. With the market over for the day, there were plenty available.

The policeman who had come to Lyle's cottage was waiting. As soon as they joined him, he handed Lyle a small orange jacket. "I understand she was wearing this earlier today."

"So she has no coat on?" Lyle asked, concern lacing his words.

Cass shivered as much from the cold as from her fear for the little girl.

The officer's face was grim as he said, "From what her parents tell me, she's wearing a jumper, jeans and boots. We don't know if she still has gloves on or a hat, or anything like that."

"Then we need to worry about exposure as well." Cass's words were flat and to the point.

"I'll get a thermal blanket and my medical bag out of the car." Lyle wasted no time in doing so.

"May I see the jacket?" Cass reached out her hand.

The policeman handed it to her and she knelt so that Hero could get a good sniff of the clothing.

Lyle returned with a satchel on his hip, the strap across his chest. He looked at her. "Ready?"

"Yes. You have a blanket?"

He patted the satchel and clicked on a large torch.

She gave the command to find. *"Voran."*

Hero started off across the village square with his nose close to the ground. Cass followed and Lyle was close behind.

Hero led them down a side street and out into a lane. Cass remained encouraged because he acted as if he had located a scent.

Her hand stayed on the leash as they continued walking at a brisk pace. Well outside the village Hero headed off the road and onto a path.

"It looks like he's taking us to the ruins," Lyle said, walking close beside her.

Her leg began to burn as the gradient grew steeper. She would push through it; she had no choice. When she faltered, Lyle supported her with a hand on her forearm. "Let me take the lead. I know this path."

"Okay. I'll let Hero go off leash." She unclipped the dog and he moved ahead of them.

Lyle took her hand and they worked their way up the path. It became more difficult to maneuver the closer to the Heatherglen Keep ruins they climbed.

Occasionally Hero would stop and look back at them. He acted impatient for them to join him. He didn't have the same trouble with the steep terrain. Soon Cass's leg went from aching to really hurting but she wouldn't let on. She was the expert in this work. A little girl's life depended on her.

Now that the sun had gone down it was pitch black. There was no natural light from the moon. Making matters worse was the fact that clouds were rolling in. It would snow tonight.

When—if—they found the girl she could very well be hypothermic. She would need medical attention immediately. Could they find her soon enough?

Cass stumbled and Lyle caught her before she went down.

"Do you need to stop?" His concerned look touched her heart.

She shook her head. "No. We have to find her."

For a second he looked as if he were going to argue. "I don't need two patients."

"I'll keep that in mind." Cass trudged forward.

Lyle pursed his lips and nodded, then joined her.

Not soon enough for Cass they made it to the ruins. In the daylight she had no doubt the area was interesting but in the dark it had an eerie feel to it. Hero sniffed around, making a circle. Finally he stood beside a couple of huge stones and barked.

"Have you found something?" Cass said to the dog as she made her way toward him, with Lyle shining the flashlight that direction. *"Set-zen."*

The dog sat.

She and Lyle were looking into a hole.

"This was the dungeon at one time," Lyle murmured.

"Looks about as much fun now. Do you see anything?" Cass searched while being careful not to lean over too far.

Lyle went down on this belly. He directed the light straight down.

"There she is," Cass cried. A small body lay curled on the ground, not moving.

She stepped closer and Lyle said, "Cass, careful! Don't fall in."

"How're we going to get her out?" Cass was already looking for things they could use.

"We'll call for help." Lyle pulled out his

phone. "Damn, I don't have a signal. One of us will have to go for help. But right now we're going to have to see to her. Minutes could mean the difference between life and death."

"We're going to have to get down to her somehow." Cass paused, panic filling her. The girl just couldn't die.

"I'll climb down." Lyle was already in the process of removing his bag.

"It looks too slick to do that. You'll have to lower me. I'm the lighter of the two of us. We can use the strap on your bag. It might not be long enough, but it'll get me close enough to drop the rest of the way."

"What about your leg? It might not hold up under that kind of pressure." Everything in Lyle's voice said that he wasn't going to agree to her plan.

Cass faced him. "That's just a chance I'll have to take. You know the path back better than me. The girl needs help now. I'm not going to argue about it anymore."

The determination in her voice must have got through to Lyle because he started unclipping the strap from his bag. With it removed, he pushed the extender so that the strap was as long as possible. "You ready?"

Cass took an end of the strap, wrapping it around her hand. "I am."

They both moved to the side of the hole. Lyle shined the light into the hole.

"There's still no movement." Cass's chest tightened. They had to get to her soon. Was she gone already?

Lyle dropped the flashlight into the hole giving them some light to work with. He then wrapped the strap around his hand just as Cass had done. She lay on her belly and crawled backward, going feet first into the hole. Lyle went to his knees, holding her under her arms as she slipped over the side.

"Feel for footholds." His voice was tight from the effort of holding her.

She did as Lyle instructed and located one. It was near the foot of her injured leg. She couldn't let the pain that shot through her slow her progress. She had to keep moving. When she was completely over the side she hung onto the strap as Lyle lowered her. She went further into the dark abyss. Thinking she had gone as far as possible, there was a sudden jerk and she was lowered further. Lyle must be on his stomach with his arms extended. She could only imagine the strain holding her was putting on his shoulder muscles. Guessing she was only a few feet from the ground, Cass let go.

She fell, hitting the ground. Pain that made

her clench her jaw rocketed through her leg. She rolled onto her hip. "Huh."

"Cass?" Lyle's fear-filled voice came from above her.

"I'm fine. Harder landing than I anticipated." Cass picked up the flashlight and crawled over to the girl. She still hadn't moved. Worry leaped in Cass. Was she already gone? No, she wouldn't believe that.

Placing two fingers to the girl's neck, Cass found a pulse, but it was weak. The child's skin was icy to the touch. Hypothermia had set in. Pulling off her jacket, she wrapped it around the girl. Cass removed her hat and scarf and put them on the girl as well.

"Cass, move far to one side so I can throw the bag down. I want vitals before I leave."

"Ready." A few seconds later Lyle's bag landed with a flop a couple of feet from her.

"Check her temperature and let me know what it is. Also, can you tell if anything is broken?" Lyle was giving her more orders than she could carry out at once. He was in full doctor mode.

Cass pulled the bag to her. Searching through it, she found the thermometer. Cass positioned the flashlight so that it shone on the girl. Thankfully Lyle had a battery-powered tympanic thermometer that Cass could just push into the girl's ear. Removing the girl's clothing would only make things worse. At least she wasn't wet.

Hero barked.

"Bleib!" Cass yelled and the dog stopped barking. *"Braver hund."* She called up to Lyle's shadow as she spread out the thermal blanket. "Temp is ninety degrees Fahrenheit—that's 32 degrees Celsius. Pulse is weak. Skin pale and cold to touch. Her breathing is shallow. I'm wrapping her in a blanket now."

"Can you do a BP?" There was an anxiousness to his voice.

"I'd rather not remove the warmth I've already given her."

"Aye. There's no question she has hypothermia."

Cass lay down on the thermal blanket and pulled the girl to her then wrapped the shiny, crinkly material around them. Maybe her body heat would help some.

Lyle's voice rang out again. "There are two heat packs in the bag. Squeeze them and put them under her arms. Don't put them against her skin."

She already knew that from her own training, but Lyle could only be frustrated by not being in the hole and the one taking care of the patient. He was a hands-on type of doctor.

"I'm leaving to call for help. Please don't take any chances. Stay put. I'll be back as soon as I can."

"Hurry."

"I will. Cass? I want your promise you won't do anything foolish." Lyle's worry laced every word.

Cass's heart swelled. He was such a good man. "Hero will be here. We'll be waiting for you."

"I'm counting on that."

Lyle hated to leave Cass but he had no choice. He had to go for help. They needed more than his to-go medical bag to save the girl's life. She needed hospital care. Right away.

Without his flashlight the walk down the rocky narrow path was slow, frustrating and dangerous. The fact that it had started sleeting only added to the difficulty. Despite that he had to keep moving. Not just for the girl's sake but for Cass's as well.

Lyle stopped often to see if he had a cell-phone signal. Everything in him pulled at him to return to Cass. As brave as she was, she still must be frightened in that black hole with a child close to death. Lyle worked his way down the hillside. He had no idea how far he would have to go before he found a signal but it couldn't be soon enough for him.

The weather was taking a turn for the worse. To complicate the conditions, the ground was slick, the path narrow and the rocks numerous. Could the situation get more dangerous?

His heart jumped when the phone connected and started ringing. Finally. The police officer answered. Lyle told him where they were and that they had found the girl. He then gave him instructions to call the hospital in Fort William and have the ambulance sent. Also, to call the clinic for the medical van. They would meet the ambulance. Every second counted. The girl might not make it if she didn't get to the hospital right away.

Lyle wasted no more words and started climbing up the hill once again. More than once he slipped as the sleet grew harder. Before he reached the ruins the sirens of help could be heard, filling the air. On flat land again at the top, he ran to the hole. Hero was still obediently sitting beside it.

"Cass!" There was no answer. "Cass?" Still nothing. Fear washed through him. What had happened to her? Had a rock fallen and hit her? All kinds of horrible scenarios played like a movie through his head. He couldn't lose Cass. He yelled louder. "Cass!"

"I'm here." Her voice wasn't strong, but it was there.

Relief flooded him as if a dam had broken.

She turned on the flashlight and pointed it toward him. "I hope help is on the way. I know now why the dungeon was the least favorite place in a castle."

Lyle chuckled. "Help is on the way. Has there been any movement out of the girl?"

"No. But let me take her temp."

He waited impatiently for her report.

"It's ninety-one Fahrenheit—a little under thirty-three Celsius."

"That's progress." He would take that. "How're you doing?"

"I'd rather be cuddled up next to you."

Lyle's heart melted. He wished that too. He was in love with Cass, he realized. "Honey, I promise you I'll make that happen just as soon as I can."

"Promise?"

"You have my word on it." When he got his arms around Cass again he might never let her go.

The sounds of people hurrying up behind him drew his attention. "Over here." A group of six people headed his way. "They're down here. In this hole."

"They?" one of the rescue men asked.

"Yes. A friend of mine, a woman who works in search and rescue. I lowered her down." Guilt pricked him. He should have gone. "We'll need a rope. I'll go down."

"You're staying put. We'll need your skills up here when we get them up." Les McArthur, the leader of the group and a man Lyle had known all his life, said, and pointed to a spot near the dog. "You stand there out of the way. What's the name of the woman in the hole?"

Lyle didn't like the idea of not being the one in charge but he did as he was told, knowing his friend was right. Still, that didn't calm his nerves. "Cass."

One of the men dropped a bag on the ground and unzipped it. He pulled a rope ladder out. Securing it to a large slab of stone, once part of the keep, he dropped it into the hole.

Les walked to the edge. "Cass, it's Les McArthur. We're coming down. Rope ladder first."

"Okay."

Lyle watched as Les went over the side. Behind him was a man with a foldup stretcher strapped to his back. Soon a bright light shone from the hole. Apparently Les had a portable light in the pack on his back.

"We're going to need ropes down here," someone called from inside the hole.

Another man pulled ropes out of a bag.

Lyle shifted from side to side, not just to keep warm but in his need to do something active. "Can I help?"

"No, this will go a lot faster if you let us do our part. Then you can do yours," one of the men said. "They're going to be fine."

Cass had better be. The girl as well.

The men threw the ropes in. A few minutes later Les called up, "Ready."

Everything in Lyle wanted to go down into that hole to Cass. Instead he stood watching all that was happening with his hands fisted at his sides and shoulders braced against the sleet-filled wind that was blowing harder by the minute.

Slowly the men started hauling the rope up. Soon the stretcher with the girl on it was being laid on the ground. At her feet was his medical bag. Cass had made sure he would have what he needed. She impressed him more every day.

"Let me check her pulse. I need to tell the hospital what to prepare for." Lyle went down on his knees beside the stretcher. He wasn't going to stand on the sidelines any longer.

The child was wrapped up in the thermal blanket. On her head was Cass's hat and around her neck was her scarf. Lyle pulled a section of the blanket back. And there was her coat. Cass had nothing to protect her from the elements.

With two fingers, he checked the child's pulse. He found it, but it wasn't easy to locate. The girl needed to leave for the hospital now. As much as he hated it, he had to trust that Les would take care of Cass. His next call after the ambulance would be to Charles and Flora. They'd also see to Cass. But he wouldn't be satisfied until he had her in his arms again.

He quickly stood, putting his bag under his arm. Giving the hole that Cass hadn't emerged from a longing look he said, "Let's get her down the hill. There's no time to waste."

Cass's body shook violently. She was so cold. Where was she? In a damp, dark, freezing hole.

No, that wasn't right. She had been cold, down to her bones. Now she was in a soft place, huddled in warmth. Her eyes flickered open. It was dark outside and a fire burned in the fireplace. She could see the flames reflecting off the wall. That was the only light in the room. Her room at the castle.

She turned her head to find Lyle asleep in a chair too small for him next to her bed. He was close enough to reach out and touch. His hair was tousled, as if he had run his fingers through it more than once. He snored softly. He must be exhausted.

The last thing she had a clear memory of at the ruins was the men securing the girl to the stretcher. She'd been so cold that all she'd been able to think about was sleeping. One of the men had given her a blanket but that hadn't stopped the cold from seeping deeper. She vaguely remembered her teeth chattering as she'd stumbled down the hill with the help of one of the rescuers.

Lyle hadn't been there when she'd come out of the hole. She'd known he wouldn't be. He would be with the girl, as he should have been. Still, that didn't mean she hadn't missed having his arms around her or his heat. It would have been preferable to those of a stranger, no matter how nice they were.

At the bottom of the hill a police car had been waiting. She'd climbed into the rear seat and the officer had turned the heat up high. Despite that, she had been bitterly cold and in a daze when she'd arrived at the castle. Charles and Flora had been waiting for her in the foyer.

"Lyle called us. Gave us strict orders to give you a full examination," Charles had said, pushing a wheelchair over to her.

Cass had been glad to see it, despite saying, "I don't think all that's necessary."

"Lyle does. And based on what he told us, you earned our attention. Thanks for what you did," Flora had added.

"Hero?" Cass had mumbled as Charles had pushed her and Flora had walked beside her.

"Esme is seeing to him. One of the police officers took him to the center. I understand he's going to get an extra helping of food. Esme said she could use a person with your skills at the center."

Cass had gone in and out of awareness while Charles had been examining her. When he'd finished, Flora had taken her turn, flexing and contracting her arm and leg. "We need to increase your therapy a bit for a few days, but I don't see why you can't be discharged on time."

Cass looked at Lyle. Discharged. At one time, all she'd wanted to do was to get home. That day would be here soon. Flora hadn't given her a specific date yet, but it was coming. Her leg and arm were much better. Despite all her efforts not to become involved, it had happened. It would be hard to leave Lyle. But she must.

She'd arrived with her emotions in a jumble and they weren't in any better shape now. In fact, her feelings for Lyle had only added to the issues. He deserved better than a woman who was so messed up. How did she even know the feelings she had for him were real? Maybe she was just reacting to her need to have someone care about her in a weak moment. That wasn't fair to him.

It didn't matter. After all, they had agreed only to a good time while she was here. Lyle hadn't said anything about wanting more. She'd made it clear she didn't. So what was she worrying about? She would leave as planned. He understood that. She would be home for Christmas.

But what if Lyle asked her to stay? Would she?

She couldn't. Heavens, she didn't know what she wanted. Taking a chance on them being together would be like jumping off a ledge. They didn't really know each other. What if it was just sexual attraction? It was best for Lyle to think of what they'd had as a nice friendship and let him move on.

It would be better for her as well. She'd learned last night that doing search and rescue was too emotionally hard for her. If that little girl had died, she would have as well. So what would she do now to make a living? Where would she end up living? There were too many unknowns.

Cass shifted. That was enough to wake Lyle. "Hey."

He sat straighter in the chair. Wrinkles filled his forehead as he studied her. "How're you feeling?"

"Better." She looked toward the window. "It's not morning?"

"No, it's still early. Do you need anything?" He leaned toward her, studying her.

"A hot bath."

"That I can handle." Lyle got to his feet.

Cass was confident he could handle almost anything.

"Let's get you into the bath. While you're there I'll go down and brew you some tea."

She grinned. "There it is again. The cure-all, but it does sound wonderful."

He started toward the bathroom. "I can tell your smart mouth isn't frozen any longer."

She giggled.

"You stay put and I'll be back for you," Lyle ordered.

"I can walk."

"Maybe so, but I'd like to carry you."

She would enjoy that. Seconds later water began running into the bath. The sounds of Lyle opening and closing cabinet doors soon followed. In a few minutes he returned to her.

"I know you've been sitting here thinking

how you could walk in there by yourself but it's not going to happen." His accent became more pronounced when he was trying to make a point.

"You don't know me well enough to know what I'm thinking."

He put his palms on the bed and leaned in close enough that his nose almost touched hers. "Then deny it."

She met his gaze with a smirk. "I do. I was actually thinking how much I'd enjoy being in your arms."

Lyle's look turned to one of bewilderment as he continued to stare at her. It quickly changed to one of pleasure that included a smile spreading across his face. "Then we have a plan."

Cass pushed the covers back. Lyle placed an arm around her waist and under her legs then lifted her against his chest. The overlarge T-shirt she wore slipped up, exposing her thigh. Lyle's hand was warm and sure on her skin. She looped her arm around his shoulders and enjoyed the ride.

He sat her on the side of the tub. "Let me check the water temp before you get in."

Cass waited, watching him trail his fingers through the water. She like the tender attention from Lyle. It made her feel cherished. When had another man come close to giving her that feeling before? Never.

Jim had come the nearest, but he hadn't understood her, her job—and especially not her relationship with her dog. His idea of caring had been to tell her she should quit doing something so dangerous. He'd never appreciated what drove her. If it had been him there tonight instead of Lyle, Jim would have never trusted her enough to care for the patient while he was gone. Jim hadn't seen her as a partner, a strong person. Lyle did.

She respected him for that. Felt Lyle returned that respect. He had searched for a missing child without questioning her judgement of using a half-blind dog, then had lowered her into the hole on her directive, and cared for the girl when she'd been pulled out. Now he was looking after her. Was there anything he couldn't do?

"How's the girl doing?"

"She'll recover with a good story to tell. I understand her family went hiking up there last week. She'd lost her doll and was convinced that it was in the ruins. She went looking for it."

"I didn't see a doll." Surely she would have noticed one.

"I didn't either, so I had a new one sent to her." He said it as if it was no big deal.

"Lyle Sinclair, you're a really nice guy." She meant every word. Too nice for her to screw up his life.

"This is ready, if you are." He reached for the hem of her T-shirt and pulled it over her head.

Cass watched him but he didn't let his gaze drop below her face. He was being such a gentleman. Scooping up her feet, he placed them in the water. Cass slipped into the bath with a sigh of contentment. It rose to just below her breasts. She glanced at Lyle. His focus had fallen lower now.

"Hey." She took his hand. His gaze met hers. A flame of awareness burned in his eyes. "It feels really wonderful in here." She closed her eyes and lay back, giving him the full view.

Lyle groaned. "I'm going down for the tea. I'll be back in a few minutes."

Cass smiled, then said in her best seductive voice, "I'd much rather have you warm me up."

"I'm the administrator of this clinic. I can't be climbing into the bath with a patient." He didn't sound convinced.

"Lock the door, put out the *Do Not Disturb* sign. Live a little. Take a walk on the wild side. You know you want to." She tugged on his hand. "Mmm…it sure is nice." Cass opened her eyelids to slits. She could see the small upward curl of Lyle's lips. He was weakening. "At least kiss me."

Lyle leaned over her, his lips finding hers. She wrapped her arms around his neck and gently pulled him into the tub. Water sloshed everywhere but she didn't care and apparently neither did Lyle. She continued to kiss him as he settled around her and brought her against him, taking the kiss deeper. When they broke apart Cass pulled at his long-sleeved shirt until her hands could wander freely over his back.

"Cass, you'll be my undoing. And the end of my job if I'm not careful." He kissed the sweet spot behind her ear.

She started working on the opening of his pants.

"How am I supposed to get out of your room without being seen in soaking wet clothes?" He sounded more perplexed than angry.

She wanted him that way. Her hand brushed across his hard manhood. "You have other things to worry about right now. I'll show you a secret passage out."

"Secret, uh?"

"First things first." She gave him an open-mouthed kiss while pushing his pants over his hips.

* * *

A few days later, Lyle sat on the couch in his cottage with his arm around Cass and her cuddled under his arm and her head on his shoulder. All the lights were off except for those on the tree. It was the prettiest Christmas tree he'd ever seen. Or maybe it was because he was sharing it with Cass. Yet he sensed something was bothering her.

She had walked home with him after work but had been more quiet than usual. Normally she told him about her day or something a dog had done during her therapy. Today had been different. They had prepared dinner of soup and sandwiches, working together like a long-married couple who knew the next move of the other. Still she'd said nothing.

Was it worry over her leaving? He'd certainly spent more time thinking about it than he found comfortable. Flora had said nothing specific about planning to discharge Cass, but he and Cass both knew the time was near. He would find out before they went to bed what was going on in that busy mind of hers.

Lyle smiled to himself. He had really come out of his respectable world with Cass's stunt of pulling him into the bath. She had added excitement to his life.

Cass had helped wring out his clothes with

a grin on her face. They'd laid them to dry near the fire and climbed into her bed. Just before dawn he'd pulled the damp clothing on so he could go home and put on some dry ones. He'd shrugged into his coat, grateful it wasn't wet. Cass gave him a goodbye kiss that had been hot enough to make them both steam. He had slipped out of her room and down a back staircase, with the jubilant thought that he wouldn't be seen. The second he had put his hand on the doorknob, Charles had pulled the door open. Lyle could only imagine the dumbfounded look on his face at that moment. Charles often came in early, but Lyle hadn't realized he used the side door.

"Hey. Aren't you going the wrong way?" Charles looked beyond him as if searching for something going on.

"I was sitting up with Cass." And other things. Very nice things.

Charles's forehead wrinkled with concern. "I checked her out last night. She seemed fine. Was something wrong?"

"No, I just wanted to make sure she was okay." Lyle made to step to past him. All he wanted was to get home and change his clothes.

A look of understanding came to Charles's

face along with a grin. He gave Lyle a pointed look. "And is she?"

"She is."

Charles continued to block the opening. "Glad to hear it. Cass is a really special person. I heard what happened and how she jumped in to help."

Lyle couldn't agree more. Cass was very special. "She is special."

"Freya did you wrong. Not every girl will." Charles's words were said softly but matter-of-factly. "Maybe it's time to give someone else a chance."

Lyle had been thinking the same thing. "You're one to be talking."

"Just because I'm a bachelor it doesn't mean you should be one. Just think about it." Charles slapped Lyle on the shoulder as he went by. "Are you wet?"

Apparently his fingers had touched Lyle's shirt. "I fell in the bath."

He heard the roll of Charles's laughter as he hurried out the door.

Cass shifted beside him now. "What're you thinking about?"

He gave her shoulders a squeeze. "I was just thinking about Charles catching me leaving the other morning."

Cass smiled against him. "So he knows about us?"

"Yes. But he would anyway. The Laird knows everything that's going on in his domain."

"Do you mind?" She turned to look up at him.

"Mind? Why would I? You're wonderful, smart, beautiful, fun to be around. Why should I mind? I'm honored."

She shifted to face him and gave him a gentle kiss. "Thank you. That was a nice thing to say."

"I meant every word."

Lyle did. He wanted more moments like this with Cass. If the truth be known, he wanted her forever. Yet he wanted to do it right this time. Make no mistake. For him there could be no long-distance relationship. He didn't want to feel pressured to ask her to stay, because they would soon be separated. But could he let her go without letting her know he cared?

Cass moved away from Lyle, then turned to face him. They had to talk. She'd put it off while they'd walked to his place, through dinner, and now she had to tell him. It shouldn't be this hard—after all they had an agreement. She'd made it clear where she stood. So why was she having such a difficult time bringing up the subject?

"What's wrong, Cass? Tell me."

She clasped her hands in her lap. "I can't hide anything from you. You always read me so well. Flora said this afternoon she plans to discharge me in three days. I can start making travel arrangements. I'll be home for Christmas."

Lyle studied her a moment before he said, "I knew the time was coming. We both did."

"Yes, we did."

He had sounded resigned, while she was a ball of growing sadness. It should be easier than this.

There was a pause as if Lyle was considering what he was going to say. "If I asked you to stay, would you?"

Cass slowly shook her head. "It's a nice thought, but not realistic."

"What about it isn't realistic?"

Her chest tightened. "My life is a mess. I don't even know what I want to do for a job now. My emotions are everywhere. I fear I've used you because you were nice to me and I had no one else to turn to. I can't make a life-changing decision like staying here with you based on that. It might not end well and you deserve better."

"We can figure it all out together." His words were said softly, beseechingly.

"Lyle, I've enjoyed every minute. Well, almost every one of them." She made an attempt at humor, but his serious look didn't change. "But I have to figure out my life on my own, otherwise it would never work."

"It seems to me it's been working great up until now." He sounded mystified that she might not think the same.

"I'm just so confused. My feelings are so jumbled up right now. I have a poor history of keeping relationships alive. I'd never want to do to you what Freya did. You're a wonderful man who shouldn't be treated that way. I can't take the chance that you become like the other men in my life, and I disappoint you. I couldn't stand to see that look on your face."

Lyle watched her for a moment. There was grief in his eyes. "Do you really believe all that rubbish? After all we have shared?"

"We're good together in bed, but that was never supposed to last forever. We talked about this when we started out." She waved a hand between them. "We had an agreement. You can't change the rules now."

"The hell I can't. Why can't you call this what it is? A relationship. I care about you. I think you feel the same about me."

"And let's just say that I do, then what? I still live in America. I may return to a job that takes me all over the world. Anytime, day or night. Or what if I decide to do something else and it's still the States? Do you think we have a chance at a long-distance romance? How did that work out for you last time?"

He flinched. "There will be no long-distance relationship between us."

"So you plan to move to America to be with me?"

His face fell. "We can work something out."

She hated what she was doing to him. That she was pushing him away. "What I'm hearing is that you want me to give up everything and come here to you."

"Put that way, it sounds unfair. Still, I think we have something real here. Something that doesn't come along often in a lifetime. Come on, Cass, stop hiding behind your fear. It's easy to keep a wall up, it's harder to let go, start again. Stop being dishonest with yourself."

"Dishonest! Like you are with your father? Have you ever made it clear to him that you don't want to return to the army? Even tried to make it clear he can accept that or not, but it won't change things? That you want him to be happy, but not at the cost of your own happiness?"

Lyle looked at her as if she had slapped him. "It's complicated."

"And my issues aren't? I'm sorry. I shouldn't have said that. You and your father's issues are none of my business. But what I do know is that if you return to active duty for someone other than yourself you will be miserable. Do you really think that's what your father wants for you?"

Lyle stood. "You're right, my issue with my father isn't any of your business. It has nothing to do with us."

"I'm not sure that's true. Here you are, asking me to stay with you, yet you might be going off to who knows where with the army. What am I supposed to do? Sit here waiting for you? I thought that was the kind of relationship you didn't want. It seems to me that we both need to make some major decisions in our lives before we involve someone else in them."

The ferocity seemed to go out of him like air from an air-bag. "All I want to do is make his last days happy ones."

"I know. But is re-enlisting the right way to do that? Or would the truth be better? You deserve to be happy as well. If you make him happy, you won't be. I know for a fact you're valuable to the clinic and this area. That you're happy with the work you do now. You're thinking of making a decision, a life-altering one, based on emotion. That's not a good way to do things. I can't do that. My decisions have to be based on more than hot sex with a handsome doc. I need to think. Need to regroup." She hated to hurt him but one of them had to think rationally. "I think it's best we leave this as a nice interlude."

"Interlude," he growled with eyes blazing—and not in the way she would have liked. "An interlude. I see."

What did he see? Lyle made the word sound nasty, ugly. "That's what we said it would be."

"If that's the way you feel then I wish you the best. Since this *interlude* appears to be over, I should escort you back to the clinic." He walked into the hall and took her coat off the hook.

Cass didn't see Lyle again until three days later when she was getting into the taxi that would take her to Fort William to start her trip home. She'd cried into her pillow each night since their breakup as loneliness consumed her, then worked hard not to show her sorrow during the day. Still, she felt she had done the right thing, for both of them.

She looked longingly at Lyle. Her heart thumped in her chest. If he asked her to stay again, would she? She needn't have worried. He remained near the front door, watching her without a smile or raising a hand in farewell.

Cass closed the car door. As she rode away, she swiped at her cheek. Unable to resist one last look, she turned to see the steps empty. Lyle had gone back inside.

If the last three days had been awful, leaving Lyle was truly horrible. What would the next week or month, or her life be like when she was thousands of miles away from him? She couldn't count the number of times she'd told herself, "Stay strong."

What she had planned not to do she had done. She'd let herself take the chance of caring again. She had fallen for Lyle.

CHAPTER TEN

LYLE HAD LET Cass's words fester. He was hurt that she could so easily dismiss what he held as precious. He now understood the meaning of "It cuts like a knife." Cass's words that night had done just that. Over time he had examined them. She was right.

He had been unfair. She'd come to Heatherglen hurt and traumatized. Only a few weeks later he was making demands on her. Had he completely forgotten everything but his own needs? Cass *should* be upset with him. They both had issues to deal with before they could commit.

Lyle didn't plan to give up. He'd give her until January then he'd go after her. Surely they could find a compromise between their lives? He loved her, and he believed she loved him. There was no way he'd misread all those touches, looks and how they felt when they came together. He couldn't be that wrong.

The woman he wanted to share his life with would not only love him but support him. Cass had proved to know him better than he knew himself. She understood who he was. More than that, she complemented him. She had strength, confidence, and the largest heart of anyone he knew.

Cass was the one for him. Of that he had no doubt.

He needed to be worthy of her. Part of being that was breaking away from his father's expectations. He had only considered his father's wishes when he'd first joined the army. No matter how sick his father was now, it was time for Lyle to concentrate on his own desires. He'd lived under his father's demands for too long. Through the clinic Lyle was providing quality and necessary care for people who needed it. He was proud of that service. It didn't matter if his father felt the same way or not.

It was past time to have a frank discussion with his father. Really talk. Not dance around the issue but make it clear the direction he intended his life to go. It was with that intention Lyle drove to his parents' house that evening.

His mother opened the door. She looked surprised and pleased to see him. She glanced around him. "Is Cass with you?"

Lyle's chest tightened at the reality that she was actually thousands of miles away. He reminded himself that he would soon be going after her. "No, she was discharged and has gone home. She asked me to say goodbye to you." Cass had. Just before she'd told him the same at the castle door and had gone inside.

His mother placed a comforting hand on his arm. "I'm sorry. I could tell you really liked her."

Lyle did. More than that, he loved her. "I hope she'll come back."

"If she is as smart as I think she is, she will." His mother gave him a quick hug.

Lyle gave her a wry smile. "Is Dad home? I wanted to talk to him for a few minutes."

"He's inside, watching TV."

Lyle took a step and stopped. "How's he feeling today?"

Her look turned to one of slight concern. "He's having a good day."

"I'm glad." Lyle started toward the living room again.

"Would you like to stay for dinner?" his mother asked.

"I'll let you know in a few minutes after I've spoken to Dad." Lyle didn't look at his mother. He was sure her mouth was drawn with concern.

Lyle walked into the living room with his shoulders squared in determination. His father was watching TV. "Hi, Dad."

"Hello. This is an unexpected visit."

Lyle took a seat on the sofa instead of the closer chair so that the two of them faced each other. "Dad, I need to discuss something with you."

He turned off the TV. "Are you here to tell me you've signed up for active duty?" His delight showed clearly on his face.

"About that. Dad, I'm not going to go on active duty by choice ever again."

That joy on his father's face quickly turned to disappointment.

"I have a good job here. I'm needed and I believe I'm respected. Army life isn't for me. It never really was. I did it for you. That's not how I want to live my life. I need to do what I love and that's medicine here, at the clinic. I'm sorry if I'm disappointing you. I've known this for a long time and I've only led you to believe that I might one day go on active duty again to make you happy, and for that I apologize."

His father's look had darkened as Lyle spoke. He leaned forward and put his elbows on his knees and clasped his hands together. His expression didn't waver. Lyle knew that one well from his childhood days when he was in trouble. "I can't say that I am pleased with your decision. It's in our family's blood to be career soldiers. I brought you up to think that way as well."

"You did. But I love private medicine more. I want to serve in another way."

His father settled back, looking both old and tired. "I see that now. I guess I didn't want to before. I grew up with my father stressing that our family fought for people by serving in the armed forces. I was given no choice, my father wasn't given one either. But we were both happy with our lots in life. It was our duty to protect. It was all I knew. All I knew to hand down to you. I never thought you would want to go another way, Lyle. I have to admit your young lady's impassioned speech did make me think, though."

Cass had done that. Lyle's ego still got a boost whenever he thought of her words.

"I heard the talk around the village about that girl going missing and what you and Cass did to save her," his father continued. "Since then others have stopped me and told me how much they appreciate you being here and the importance of the clinic. I'm proud when I hear it. I'm sorry that you're not going to return to the army but I do love you, son."

Lyle went across to his father and gave him a hug. Afterwards he called, "Mum, I'll be staying for dinner."

Cass had never known misery like the kind she'd endured on the way to the airport. Everything in her screamed to return to Lyle. But he hadn't even waved goodbye. Had she hurt him that much? She felt sick inside.

The tears had flowed the entire trip to Fort William and then on to Aberdeen. More than once the taxi driver had looked in his rear-view mirror with apprehension, but he'd said nothing.

She'd done everything she'd told herself not to. She'd let herself care. About him. The people at Heatherglen. Even Andy and that funny-looking dog, Dougal. Hero. Her emotions had been in a muddle when she had arrived at the clinic, and they weren't any better now that she'd left.

She'd known fear from when she'd almost lost her brother. She'd experienced deep loss from losing Rufus. And now Lyle was gone. This time was harder. She couldn't even breathe, the pain was so strong. Worse, she had chosen this. She wrung her hands.

She couldn't turn back. All she'd said to Lyle

was true. She needed to have her act together
before she made an emotional commitment to
anyone, especially to him. Her parents were
expecting her. It was Christmas, and they were
worried about her. She had to see them first.

What her future would look like still needed
to be decided. Search and rescue was no longer
for her. So what would she do now? There was
also her house to think about. When she had
her life in order, she'd see if Lyle still felt the
same. He deserved someone who knew what
she wanted and had her head on straight. Only
then would she return to Lyle and discuss any
future they might have.

The flight home wasn't much better emotionally than her ride to the airport. She'd only
found relief in the few hours she had slept. Her
parents were there to meet her. They quickly
enveloped her in tight hugs. She needed those
more than anything at the moment. They insisted that she go to their house for dinner and
stay the night. Cass didn't resist. Right now
she wanted their circle of security. With them
she could just be, not think. She needed time
to regroup.

Her parents' home was decorated for Christmas. Cass should have expected that. The minute she looked at their tree, her eyes filled with
tears. It was all light, tinsel and glitter. It made

her appreciate the simple, natural tree that stood in Lyle's living room. More than that, she wanted Lyle.

Her brother and his family came for supper the next day. With two young children, the meal was lively. Cass was glad to see them but she was so exhausted, both mentally and physically, that she excused herself early. Despite all the tears she'd shed during the day, she still wanted a good cry. She hurried to her childhood bedroom and closed the door. Minutes later she was in the shower, letting those banked tears flow.

By the time there was a knock on the door she was in bed. "It's Mom. Can I come in?"

"Yes."

Her mother entered, carrying a mug. "I brought you some tea. I thought it was too late for coffee."

That was enough to have Cass's eyes swimming once more. She'd never cried this much in her entire life. Never been this distraught. The idea she might never have a chance to share time with Lyle again had her emotionally splintered. She had to get control of herself. Showing her emotions like this wasn't her. But, then, much about her over the last few weeks was different. Like pulling Lyle into the tub. That had been so much fun, for a number of reasons.

Her mother set the tea on the bedside table then perched on the edge of Cass's bed. "I had no idea you hated tea so much, or is something else going on? What're you not telling us? Are you still in pain?"

Cass hated the fear she heard in her mother's voice. "I told you everything about my injury. I promise I'm much better. It's my heart that's broken. And I think I'm the one who broke it." She poured out her sorrow and what had happened while she'd been at Heatherglen.

Her mother held her while she cried. When she settled down her mother said, "So what're your plans now, honey?"

"I don't know. Tomorrow morning I'm going to call about my job. I'm going to resign from it. That work isn't for me anymore."

Her mother patted her leg. "Your dad will be pleased to hear that. We've worried about you being in all those far-flung places by yourself for too long."

Cass hadn't been by herself. Rufus had been with her. Now she had no one. "I've been thinking that I might enjoy training rescue dogs instead."

"That sounds like something you'd be good

at. And what about that amazing doctor of yours?"

Hers? She hoped despite how she had left things between her and Lyle that he would at least speak to her when she saw him again. "Mom, he asked me to stay. I was afraid to make such a big decision when I was so messed up over being hurt, Rufus dying and not being closer to home. I didn't know what I wanted my future to look like then. I hurt him badly. I'm not sure he'll ever want me again."

"So, do you know how you feel now?" Her mother held her hand.

"I knew the minute I left the clinic. I wouldn't let myself turn around, though. I needed to come home. To see you and Daddy." Cass looked directly at her mother. "I love him."

"Then I suggest you go back and tell him."

Cass murmured, "I don't know if he wants me anymore. He didn't even say goodbye."

"Honey, if all you've told me is true, I wouldn't worry about that. He wants you. I'd suggest you take care of business here as soon as possible then go tell him how you feel and see what happens."

"I don't know…"

She mother stood. "Our family knows better than most how easily something can be almost taken away. Grab every chance at happiness and have no regrets."

The one thing Cass had been with Lyle was happy—and at Heatherglen, too. "What about Christmas?"

Her mother shrugged. "We'll celebrate it early. Or late." Then she grinned. "Or come to Scotland."

"Oh, Mom." Cass wrapped her arms around her mother. "I love you."

Over the next few days Cass resigned from her job, packed her bags and closed up her house. She was on her way to find that happiness she wanted. And that started with Lyle.

Christmas had never really mattered to Lyle. Cass had managed to make it exciting for a while, but that had gone with her. He'd spent the last week going through the motions. To say he wasn't in a festive mood would be an understatement.

He was actually heading into the worst Christmas of his life. It was going to top the year Freya had left him, and the one when his father wouldn't speak to him because he'd said he was going inactive so he could take the job helping Charles get the clinic started.

Losing Cass was like losing an arm or a leg. He had to relearn how to function without her.

Every day he forced himself to do what was necessary. People were starting to notice. The few times he had seen his parents his mother had watched him with worry and hugged him a little tighter than normal. Even Charles had made a smart remark about Lyle not looking as cheerful dry as he had wet. Lyle had snarled and stalked way.

No, Christmas couldn't go by fast enough for him. He was living for the new year. Surely he and Cass could sort something out? Find a way they could be together? If he had to leave Heatherglen and follow her all over the world, then so be it.

Now he was doing his duty as the doctor on call at the Christmas-tree lighting in the village square. He remained on the outside of the crowd around the huge tree. It was dark except for the interior lights of the businesses that surrounded the square.

As soon as he was no longer needed he would slip away to his cottage, even though he found no solace there. His home held too many memories of Cass. Their tree still stood in the living room. More than once he'd thought of taking it down but he couldn't bring himself to do it despite the fact it was a daily reminder of Cass.

Lyle stuffed his hands in his coat pockets

and focused on Charles giving his Laird of Heatherglen annual Christmas speech. It was the only time Lyle smiled because he was well aware of how much Charles disliked being in the spotlight.

A movement in front of him and to the right caught Lyle's attention. *Cass?* He shook his head. For him she was like the ghost of Heatherglen. More than once he had walked around a corner and thought he'd glimpsed her. Or walked by the lounge and heard her voice. Each time he'd had to calm his rapid heartbeat as disappointment had set in. He had to remind himself she was in America.

He had laid out a plan, one he would adhere to. She would have the space and time she needed to think, and process what she wanted. Lyle was determined to give her that, even if it killed him. In January he would go after her. From there they would figure out what their future together would look like.

The person continued toward him. Lyle narrowed his eyes in the hope of seeing better. Despite his efforts not to let his heart race or hold his breath in anticipation, it didn't work. Still, in the dim light he couldn't make out any facial features.

It was a woman. She came nearer. Her walk

was so much like Cass's. She held herself just as Cass did. Was his mind playing tricks on him?

Finally, she stepped close enough that he could see a scarf around her neck and a hat on her head like the one Cass had bought from his mother. Lyle remained still, sure she was a figment of his imagination.

It wasn't until she said, "Hello, Lyle," that he let himself believe and breathe. His heart raced as if he were running. It was Cass! She'd come back. Was really here. Unable to move, he stood there in disbelief.

She closed the distance between them. "Lyle?"

He put one foot in front of the other and grabbed her, pulling her against his chest. Lifting her off the ground, he was rewarded with a sigh from her as her arms tightly circled his neck. Sometime later, Lyle let her slide down his body and he stepped back. The last thing he want to do was scare her off. "Cass, is it really you?"

"Yes."

"Are you okay? Is your leg okay?" He gave her a searching look.

"I'm fine." There was a smile in her voice. "I just forgot something."

"Forgot something?" Now he sounded like an idiot. His hands shook in his eagerness to touch her. He shoved them in his pockets.

"Yes. You."

"Me?"

She watched him closely with a look of uncertainty. "Yeah, you. I was wondering if we could have that conversation about compromise you suggested."

"I'd like that. A *lot*." He pulled her to him again and kissed her with all the pent-up emotion he'd had to hold in check. It was a long and deep kiss.

The roar of the crowd broke them apart. They gave each other a startled look, then grinned. The cheer had been for the Christmas tree being lit.

Lyle looked at her beautiful, much-loved face. "I'm finished here. Where're you staying?"

"I was going to stay somewhere in the village, unless I had a better offer." Cass grinned.

"You have one now. Where are your bags?" Lyle looked around.

"At the airport, I hope. Long story that I don't want to talk about now."

Smiling, he took her hand and hurried her to where his car was parked. They needed to get away before people started talking to them.

He held Cass's hand as much as the drive to his cottage would allow, afraid if he lost contact she would disappear.

As he helped her out of the car, he pulled her to him again, inhaling deeply and filling his head with her scent. "You have no idea how I've missed you."

A flutter like birds taking off filled Cass's middle. She looked at Lyle's handsome face. The one she had missed so much. "I'm glad."

"Glad?" Lyle sounded incredulous.

"Yes, I was afraid you wouldn't talk to me." She watched him for a reaction.

"Are you kidding? I'm in love with you, Cass. Nothing will ever change that."

"In love with me?" So this was what it felt like to have everything she'd ever dreamed of.

"What did you think I meant when I asked you to stay here with me?"

She lifted a shoulder in a shrug and let it fall. "I don't know. I had so much stuff going on in my head I wasn't sure what you meant."

His hands went to her shoulders. "Cass, I wouldn't have asked you to stay with me unless I meant forever."

"I should've known that. I should've heard you out. I was scared. Of myself and what you wanted."

"Come inside. We'll discuss this out of the cold. I want you to be warm and comfortable when I explain how much I love and want you." He gave her a quick kiss before he took her hand then pushed the car door closed.

Inside his cottage, Lyle helped her hang up her outer clothing. She took off her shoes, walked to the doorway of the living room and stopped. Their tree was still there.

"Is something wrong?" Lyle said from behind her.

She turned and smiled. "No, everything is perfect. I missed you and your cottage."

"I hope it was me more." There was still an unsure look in his eyes.

Cass went up on her toes and kissed him. "It was you. Almost all you."

When they separated, he called over his shoulder as he walked to the kitchen, "I'll make us some tea. We need to talk."

She liked the sound of that. They did. She needed to apologize and tell him how she felt. It was time to stop worrying about woulda, coulda, shoulda and try living. When she was around Lyle she wanted to live. She was happy. Blissfully so.

A few minutes later he offered her a mug of tea. Instead of sitting beside her, Lyle chose the chair. Cass couldn't help but pout. Maybe he was still mad at her.

"I'm sitting over here because I can't trust myself when I sit next to you. We need to talk."

Cass's heart jumped. "I know what you mean."

That brought a smile to his lips before he said, "I know I wasn't fair to you. I was so self-absorbed that I wasn't thinking about what was best for you. You were here to recover from a horrible experience, and I should've given you more room, not asked you for more than you could give. Before you left you said some things I needed to hear. I have to admit it made me angry but that didn't mean that I didn't need to hear them. Or that I didn't love you. I talked to my father. Told him in clear and concise language that I wouldn't be returning to active duty."

Cass hissed in a breath. "How did that go?"

"He didn't like it, but he accepted it. Even told me that he's proud of the work I'm doing at the clinic."

That had to have been a tough conversation for both men. She had to admire Lyle for doing it.

Lyle continued, "At least it's a positive start. I don't think he'll ever get over it but, then, I can't live my life for him. I've got to live it for me."

"You're right. That's a hard lesson I've had to learn over the last few days as well. I knew the moment I looked out the rear window of the car for you as I was going down the drive that I was leaving behind the best thing in my life. That you held the key to my happiness. I was afraid that if I took what you offered, somewhere down the road it might be taken from me. I couldn't stand the thought of that happening. What I soon learned was that trying to live without you was far worse. I love you, Lyle."

That was all it took for Lyle to come to her. He wrapped his arms around her and gave her the sweetest kiss that held a promise that he loved her too.

After they broke apart, Lyle said, "If you don't want to live here, we can live in America, or anywhere else for that matter, as long as we are together. I can practice medicine anywhere."

"Oh, no, I would never take you away from Heatherglen. Cluchlochry. You belong here. Are needed here. I've been thinking about something Flora said. She mentioned Esme could use me at the canine therapy center. I think I would like to train dogs."

"That sounds like a wonderful idea." Lyle hugged her.

"You think you could stand to have me around all the time?" She studied his face.

He chuckled. "I can't think of anything better."

"I love you, Lyle."

"I love you, Cass."

Sometime later they were lying in Lyle's large bed in each other's arms. Cass had found the place where she belonged, where she was completely happy. "You know, there's something to the Christmas pudding thing."

"How's that?" Lyle's hand caressed her bare back over her shoulders.

"I asked to be happy." She cupped his cheek. "And I am. Blissfully so."

He gave her a quick kiss. "And I wished for you to stay longer."

"Why?"

"Because I need a date for the Christmas ball!"

* * * * *

Welcome to the
Pups that Make Miracles quartet!

Highland Doc's Christmas Rescue
by Susan Carlisle
Festive Fling with the Single Dad
by Annie Claydon

Available now!

And next month, look out for

Making Christmas Special Again
by Annie O'Neil
Their One-Night Christmas Gift
by Karin Baine